It was not just a casual kiss

Releasing her mouth finally, Trent murmured persuasively. "You don't have to go, Laurel. I have a room booked. This could be quite delightful."

Her senses returned, and with them her anger. So that was his game!

"Not so fast hotshot!" she hissed angrily at him. "I'm not the pushover you seem to think! I might have guessed where that soft approach was leading, but this is as far as it goes!" She rummaged in her bag, grabbed a couple of five-pound notes and flung them at him. "That's the only way I pay for anything I've had," she declared and wrenched open the door to the frozen Siberian landscape outside.

He regarded her with lazy amusement. "Baby, it's mighty cold out there," he said softly.

Lee Stafford was born and educated in Sheffield where she worked as a secretary and in public relations. Her husband is in hospital-catering management. They live in Sussex with their two teenage daughters.

LOVE TAKES OVER
Lee Stafford

Harlequin Books

TORONTO • NEW YORK • LONDON
AMSTERDAM • PARIS • SYDNEY • HAMBURG
STOCKHOLM • ATHENS • TOKYO • MILAN

Original hardcover edition published in 1990
by Mills & Boon Limited

ISBN 0-373-17090-4

Harlequin Romance first edition July 1991

LOVE TAKES OVER

CHAPTER ONE

IT STARTED to snow not long after she left Heathfield, at first just odd, drifting flakes that she ignored as she pressed on along the deserted, winding country lane. Then the heavy grey sky darkened and snow fell in earnest, a rising wind causing it to whirl around her like white-clad dervishes.

Laurel switched on the windscreen wipers and wished too late that she had kept to the main road. She had had several calls to make and, busy all day, had been left little time to gnaw over the awful row with her adoptive father which had erupted at breakfast. Choosing a quieter, traffic-free route back would, she had felt, give her the opportunity to reflect more calmly on his decision and to prepare herself for the return home, which she did not anticipate with any pleasure. It didn't sound as though he was prepared to change his mind. And she was no more reconciled to his plans than she had been that morning.

But now here she was, caught up in a mini-blizzard, having to strain to see more than a few yards ahead, and needing all her concentration to keep the wheels from slipping on the suddenly treacherous road surface. And, to make matters worse, the car's engine was making a weird noise, as if it was having to struggle to keep going at all.

The clock on the dashboard showed four-thirty, but with Christmas only a few days away night was closing in. Miles from any town or village, with not even a farmhouse in sight, surrounded by empty, darkening fields and shadowy trees all veiled in thickly falling snow, the car finally spluttered to a halt.

Laurel sighed wearily and taking a torch from the glove compartment got out, opened the bonnet and peered in. Spark plugs? Carburettor? None of her elementary attentions succeeded in coaxing it back into action. Now, when she tried the ignition, the engine seemed quite lifeless.

Although she had lived in Sussex for all of her twenty-one years, that did not mean she was familiar with every back road or byway. The road she was on now was not one she had used often, and although she knew where she was, more or less, it didn't help a lot. It would be a long hike back to the main road, she decided, studying her map by torchlight. Better to push on ahead. It looked as if there might be an inn a few miles along the road, and even if it was closed, she could bang on the door and beg the use of the phone.

Locking up the car and pulling on her gloves, Laurel set off determinedly along the dark, empty road. Her sheepskin jacket was warm but more suitable for driving than walking, since it was only three-quarter-length. Her boots were leather, but they were fashion footwear, not intended for trudging through snow, and she was, not surprisingly, hatless, flakes settling on her thick dark hair, which was very soon soaked.

There was no one about—perhaps as well, she thought with a brief shudder which she forcibly controlled. Somewhere a predatory owl hooted, a ghostly sound in the swirling whiteness around her. Scuffles in the leafless hedgerows probably only meant a hunting fox, but were disconcerting all the same. The loneliness was oppressive, and Laurel gulped, fighting her way through snow which prevented her from seeing more than a few steps in front of her at a time.

This morning she had woken up reasonably content, she thought wretchedly. She had a secure future, a devoted family, work she loved, and it was almost Christmas. Then her father had casually announced that he was selling the company forthwith—no arguments, no compromise. And now she was lost in the snow, in the middle of nowhere. She was in limbo, and so was her entire life.

She shone the torch ahead, its feeble beam no competition for the elements, and forced her mind away from the desperate sense of betrayal that Robert Ashby could do such a thing, knowing how it would affect her. Right now she had a more immediate predicament. She had to find civilisation of some kind and phone for assistance. However awful the prospects seemed, she had no wish to die of exposure after a night out on the snow-covered approaches to the Downs.

The inn which the map had shown as only a few miles from where she had stopped seemed no closer after she had walked for nearly an hour. The snow was a good inch thick on the ground by now, and her feet were frozen, although fortunately the leather boots had so far kept them dry. But Laurel was beginning to feel the onset of panic. Had she read the map correctly? Could she perhaps have passed the inn in the darkness, without seeing it? Not one vehicle had overtaken her all the time she was walking, and she was not sure whether to be relieved or disappointed by that.

Real fear had started to knot her stomach when at last she thought she saw a glimmer of light in the distance. At first she wasn't sure she hadn't imagined it, or that it wasn't merely wishful thinking, and she stumbled towards it, slightly breathless as she realised on a surge of relief that it was not the result of a hallucination.

A country pub, lights blazing from its windows, and a number of cars drawn up outside—thank heaven for the new all-day opening laws, Laurel thought ruefully as she pushed open the heavy oak doors and almost fell inside, driven by a blast of icy wind.

The bar was full of people, laughing, drinking, all dressed up, obviously for a festive occasion. The scents of a turkey dinner lingered on the air, competing with those of coffee and cigar tobacco. Coloured lights winked along the oak beams, tinsel was looped across the ceiling, and in one corner a huge, brightly decorated Christmas tree held pride of place, twinkling with baubles. In the large old-fashioned fireplace, logs crackled and flames reached halfway up the chimney. The warmth enveloped Laurel as she stood by the door, and, grateful for it as she was, the contrast with the cold outside almost made her faint.

The merrymakers glanced curiously at the girl in her snow-covered jacket, her wet dark hair plastered to her head and straggling over her shoulders, an apparition at the feast. Shedding melted snow on the carpet, she made her way to the bar, and only then became aware of the man watching her more intently than the others, who had returned to the business of enjoying themselves.

Obviously not one of their party, he was half seated on a bar stool, long legs clad in well-pressed grey flannel trousers stretched out in front of him, one arm resting negligently on the counter, while the other hand swirled the contents of his glass. Beneath each sleeve of his grey jacket an inch of immaculate cuff gleamed white, fastened by a cufflink of gold and jet.

Laurel registered these impressions through a haze of heat and tobacco and light which made the room dip and sway alarmingly. She clutched at the polished surface of the bar and shook her head slightly, defying the sudden dizziness that threatened her.

A steadying hand closed over hers, and the gold and jet cufflink swam back into focus as the man beside her said, 'Landlord, I think you'd better give the young lady a brandy.'

The voice was clear and calmly authoritative, but difficult to place. There was just a suggestion of an accent that might have been American or Canadian, a faint transatlantic hint, but even that Laurel could not have sworn to. She looked up gratefully as the balloon goblet of amber liquid was set before her, and, since she was only five feet three, she had a long way to look. Even half seated it was easy to see he was tall, although not lanky—well put together. His face followed suit with an elegant symmetry of line, a clean, uncluttered profile and gleaming dark gold hair brushed back from a broad, intelligent brow, giving him the aura of a Renaissance prince.

Laurel took another sip of the brandy, wondering if it was responsible for the fanciful wanderings of her mind, that and the relief of coming in out of the cold, lonely darkness through which she had walked.

'All right now?' queried the Renaissance prince, who still had his hand over hers.

'Yes—thank you,' she gulped. 'I must look like the Ghost of Christmas Past, in this state! My car died on me a few miles down the road, and I had to walk here.'

He smiled, and the symmetry vanished, the wide curve of his mouth breaking up the lines into an entirely different composition. Laurel watched, fascinated, the small hollows that appeared either side of his jaw, and thought he was two people, either of whom one would instantly recognise in a crowd.

'That's a bad break. You'd better come and sit over by the fire.'

Without pausing to ask her permission he helped her out of the now dripping coat, which he draped over a chair, pulling back another one for her to sit on.

Laurel hesitated. She had never seen him before in her life and had no idea who he was. Natural caution made her demur at accepting his ministrations.

'I don't——' she began, but got no further, for he simply stood, holding out the chair and awaiting her compliance without a glimmer of doubt that it would follow. There was about him an aura of calm command, the unstressed confidence of a man who would prove unflappable and capable of making a sound, un-emotional decision in any circumstances. Surprising herself, Laurel sank into the proffered chair with the inward excuse that her own present circumstances robbed her of the strength to protest. Something about that stone wall of imperious arrogance was strangely reassuring, and she recognised the danger of confusing these two concepts which should have seemed mutually contradictory.

It isn't as if it need worry me, she told herself as he settled easily in the seat opposite her, just as the cheerful crowd in the bar burst into a loud, not altogether har-monious rendition of 'Good King Wenceslas'.

'Very appropriate,' her companion observed drily, in-dicating the snowy gloom beyond the brightly lit windows. 'It's an office party. They've been here for some time, and won't be leaving in a hurry, I imagine. Are your feet dry?'

'What? Oh…er…yes.' Laurel stretched out her booted legs towards the warmth of the fire. Divested of her coat, she was wearing a knitted suit of deep cherry red, with a Chanel-type jacket, the colour accentuating the darkness of her hair and her pale ivory complexion. Although a petite girl, she was generously curved in all the right places, and small-waisted, as the suit clearly displayed. But she was not aware of the effect created as she raised her hand to push back the wet elfin locks from her face, thinking only of what a mess she must look.

'My mother always insists one will catch a chill if one's feet get wet, for all I tell her that viruses don't operate that way,' he grinned.

'My stepmother says that too. I think it's a belief they all share,' she smiled, showing small white teeth. She was feeling better now, the warmth of the brandy, the fire, and—yes, this man's capable, reassuring manner all responsible for the thaw. Steam had begun to rise from her coat as it dried, and his deep-throated laughter rang out.

'Have you read *War and Peace*? I thought of Napoleon's soldiers trudging homewards through the endless Russian winter when you came in, covered in snow.'

Laurel grimaced. 'The retreat from Moscow? I'm afraid I was only on my way from Heathfield to Lewes! But the weather is certainly Siberian. I must find a phone and call the garage emergency service.'

'There's one on the bar,' he told her.

She was aware of his eyes following her as she rose and went to use the phone. It wasn't the lecherous observation some men considered sexy, which usually only succeeded in making most women feel grimy and re-

sentful. He appraised her, but coolly, as he might a
painting or a piece of fine china, silently totalling good
points and bad without betraying his conclusions. Con-
trarily, this steady, dispassionate regard affected her far
more strongly than an undressing stare would have done,
making her conscious of her shortcomings and her
present unappetising state.

Turning her back on him...not that it helped, since
she was still aware of his surveillance...she deliberately
set aside her disagreement with her father and phoned
home. They might be at odds, but for more than twenty
years he had loved, encouraged and cared for the girl
he had adopted privately as a baby. She owed him at
least the comfort of knowing she was safe.

It was Ana's soft Spanish voice that answered the
phone.

'Oh, *querida*, thank God! I was beginning to be afraid
when I rang the office and they said you had not yet
come back! Your father is not home at the moment.
Would you like him to fetch you when he comes in?'
Passing her driving test was a skill her father's wife had
been unable to master.

'No, it's all right. I'm in a pub, warm and dry, and
I've phoned the garage people. They'll give me a lift
back into Lewes. Don't worry.'

When she returned to the table Laurel found her glass
had been refilled, and she did not attempt to veil her
questioning glance. The first drink had been almost
medicinal. How did he know whether she wanted or
could take a second? Was he trying to get her drunk?
After all, she had no idea what might lie behind that air
of refinement.

The corners of his mouth eased upwards slightly as
he imperturbably returned her interrogative stare.

'What's the problem? I don't figure you'll be driving anywhere, and for all you're only pint-sized, you don't look to me like a lady who'd be floored by two drinks.'

'The problem is, I prefer to be asked,' Laurel said coolly, guiltily aware of sounding ungracious. But he remained untroubled.

'I have this ingrained habit of making up my own mind—and sometimes other people's too,' he said. 'What the hell? It's Christmas, after all. You and I are marooned here amid all this seasonal hilarity. We may as well make the best of it.'

The dryness of his voice indicated that, while he did not disapprove of the seasonal hilarity, neither did it concern him too much. Her brief annoyance was superseded by curiosity. Who was he? And how far was he from home at this festive time of year? Laurel sensed a mystery.

She shrugged and said, 'Well, the garage have promised to send someone, but they said I must be prepared for a long wait. I'm not the only one in this situation. But don't *you* have to be anywhere else tonight?' She had noted that his own glass had been replenished too.

The slow, fascinating smile reassembled his features again. His eyes were not blue, as might have been expected, but golden-brown, the colour of fine tawny port, and his skin had the healthy glow of someone not merely tanned from a holiday in the sun, but used to a better climate than the one in which he presently found himself.

'No, I'm staying here tonight,' he informed her. 'I pulled off the road and booked myself a room as soon as the weather turned bad. I don't care for driving through snow.'

'A white Christmas doesn't appeal to you?'

'Sure, if I'm up in the mountains somewhere, with sleighbells, *glühwein*, skating—and nothing else to do. But that's not the case. I've business in hand, and it's a damn nuisance. Still, you're a mitigating factor. Do you have a name?'

Laurel regarded him steadily, but inside her a strange, breathless excitement made her heartbeat uneven. A mitigating factor? Unromantic language, a cool, dispassionate gaze, but there was something about him which exuded masculine sexuality. He didn't advertise it—if anything, he veiled it—but it was there nevertheless. Laurel acknowledged her own dangerous mood of angry rebellion, the volatile state of her own emotions, and told herself this was *not* the time to embark on anything . . . but he was like no one else she had met before.

However, there could surely be no harm in divulging her identity? She said, 'I'm Laurel——'

He cut her off quickly.

'Laurel will do.' The brown eyes held hers hypnotically. 'First names are sufficient for ships that pass in the night, OK? I'm Trent.'

Almost as if he didn't want her to know who he was. Could he be someone famous travelling incognito? Her fine dark brows arched and knit over the delicate bridge of her nose as she gazed at him, puzzled. She didn't recognise him. Should she?

'You're an American?' she half asked, half stated, and he riposted quickly,

'What makes you say so?'

'I . . . I don't know,' she said, taken aback by his swift, blocking response. 'You sound vaguely like one, I suppose.'

He smiled faintly. 'You can't always place people by the way they sound. I've lived in America for some years, on and off. My mother's American. But this voice, like its owner, has moved around a good deal. Laurel, what do you say to having a meal? I haven't eaten, and I dare say you haven't either.'

The change of subject was undoubtedly deliberate. Slightly snubbed, she said, 'I wouldn't bank on getting served at this hour. It's too late for lunch and too early for dinner. You may have moved around a lot, but you don't know much about English pubs!'

He inclined his gleaming bronze-gold head in a mocking salute. 'I bow to your superior local knowledge. But there's a maxim I believe in—every problem is an opportunity in disguise. Are you hungry?'

'I won't deny that,' she admitted. She had eaten a sandwich in a layby at about half-past twelve, and nothing since. The notion of hot food was most enticing.

'Then let's see what can be done about it.'

Trent got up and walked over to the bar—a matter of a few easy strides, with his long legs—and leaned over it, engaging the landlord in conversation. Laurel couldn't hear what was said—the office party were by now noisily doing the hokey-cokey—but he returned wearing a triumphant smile.

'He says that lot over there won't be going anywhere until the snow lets up, so it's hardly worth his closing only to open up again in an hour or two. His wife's still in the kitchen, and she'll do us a meal, but today "it's a choice between turkey and turkey". I quote.'

Laughter she hadn't felt capable of all day bubbled up irresistibly inside Laurel.

'Oh, lord! I think I'll settle for turkey, then—how about you?' she grinned.

The meal was good, plentiful, with freshly cooked vegetables. Laurel, professional interest alerted, assessed the establishment's problems and advantages. A good, plain cook in the kitchen, but probably single-handed and hard pressed, unable to offer much in the way of choice. Caterplus, her father's company, had a good range of ready dishes which would help expand the menu. She'd make a point of arranging a working visit.

And then it hit her again. All too soon, Caterplus would no longer be her father's company. Some vast, anonymous corporation would swallow up its individuality. The new managing director would most likely be an aloof, remote automaton whom she could not readily approach with her ideas and plans, who would care nothing for staff who had worked loyally for years. The entire character of the organisation would change, from an enthusiastic, family-run operation to an unimportant cog in a vast wheel. People would be dismissed, or would become disenchanted and leave anyhow. And, in spite of Robert Ashby's assurances, she was not convinced there would be a place for her. How could he do this? How *could* he?

Trent filled her glass from the carafe of white wine.

'Hey,' he said, 'don't pull such a face! The food isn't half bad.'

Laurel shook herself and forced a smile.

'On the contrary, it's good. I was thinking of . . . of something else.'

He leaned back in his chair, the tawny eyes somnolent but watchful, like those of a great jungle cat.

'I'll say! I wouldn't care to be the person on your mind,' he said amusedly. 'You had murder in your eyes right then. Errant husband? No——' glancing down at her ringless left hand '—you're not married. Straying boyfriend?'

Laurel found herself resenting this rather patronising trivialisation of her dilemma.

'Why is it always assumed that a woman's problems have to be emotional?' she demanded crossly. 'Actually, it's nothing like that. Although a man is at the root of the trouble, he's my father.'

She swallowed a sip of wine, and all at once could hold in the rage and pain no longer. Whether the alcohol had loosened her tongue, or whether it was because she was talking to a stranger she need not meet again, she did not know—and did not very much care.

'He's selling our company,' she said angrily. 'Just like that—no discussion, no appeal. Caterplus has always been a family business; now we'll probably end up as part of some vast conglomerate who won't care a hoot for us! The staff will all hate it, and so will I! But he doesn't give a damn!'

Trent regarded her thoughtfully, but she couldn't tell if it was sympathy she read in those strange eyes.

'Hm,' he said. 'Of course, I don't know all the details, but . . . have you considered that your father might have his reasons?'

'Oh, yes!' Laurel snorted bitterly. 'Brilliant reasons! He wants to retire early and take Ana, my stepmother, somewhere warm for the winter. Of course I don't object if they push off to Barbados or Tenerife for a couple of months, but why sell out completely? We could get by without him for a while. I could hold the fort. I always imagined that one day—that——' she choked, tears springing to her expressive dark eyes, and fought to get a grip on herself.

Trent concentrated impassively on his hot mince pie and cream until she had recovered her equilibrium. Had she been less distraught, less self-involved, Laurel might have been grateful for his tact. Overwhelming her with sympathy would anyhow only have pushed her over the edge into a torrent of furious tears. All the same, she was instantly resentful when he said calmly, 'I guess that's the crux of the matter. You expected him to leave the business to you? Surely you must realise that you're full young for that kind of responsibility?'

'*Now* I am, yes, but I won't always be!' she burst out frustratedly. 'Why can't he wait a few years? He's not old, only fifty-five. If I were his *son* he'd have more concern for my future.'

Or even if I were his *real* daughter, the unspoken rider raced through her fevered mind. She couldn't tell Trent that that was the accusation she had flung at Robert that morning. All those years of feeling she was his daughter, although she had always known she was adopted, all that sense of security and being cared for that he had given her, he had whipped away from under her in a few short sentences. She wasn't really his flesh and blood, so why should he worry about passing on his business to her?

Trent, however, did not appear to sympathise with her.

'I'd say that was a mite selfish, expecting your father to postpone the retirement for which he feels, for whatever reasons, the time is right, simply to coincide with your desires. You're young, and can make your own life. And yes, if you were his son, his position might understandably be a little different.'

Laurel glowered at him. 'Oh, I see! You're one of those male chauvinists who objects on principle to women in power!'

'You misjudge me, lady,' he said, with a dry, amused smile Laurel found infuriating. 'It's not the principle I object to, it's the practice which rarely works for a woman, unless she's very determined and ruthlessly single-minded.'

'How do you know I'm not?' she countered.

He allowed his gaze to slide from the top of her dark, glossy head to the toe of her small, neat leather boots, lingering only slightly, but tantalisingly, on various points of her anatomy en route, so that she flushed uncomfortably.

'I don't know,' he said, with irritating reasonableness. 'But I will say this. All the successful businesswomen I've known have been older than you, and either dedicatedly single or past the stage where they might be side-tracked by family commitments.'

The calmer he remained, the more agitated Laurel found herself becoming, and by far the worst aspect of this was that although she knew it, although she heard herself growing shriller, she could not do anything about it.

'Yes, my father trotted out that hackneyed old objection too!' she spat at him caustically. '"You'll want to get married soon, and have babies, Laurel"!'

Trent laughed, a low, attractive chuckle that sent an unexpected tingle up Laurel's spine.

'That hackneyed old objection has a solid biological basis,' he said, with insidious softness. 'I reckon he might have a point. You look eminently nubile to me.'

The tingle spread swiftly all over her body. A table and two feet of space separated them, and he had made no attempt to touch her, but the quiet intimacy of his voice and the steady, hypnotic tawny gaze made Laurel feel that at any moment, he might. And that if he did, she would be powerless to prevent it. She wrestled fiercely against this sensation of losing control, of being somehow in his power, hating it and simultaneously wondering why it was not unpleasant.

'I have no plans for marriage. It's the last thing on my mind,' she declared firmly. 'And even if I had, why should it make any difference? No one ever suggests men shouldn't combine fatherhood and a career.'

'Be realistic, Laurel. It's an easier combination,' he pointed out. 'You must admit that you'd complicate your life by trying to do two difficult things well. Is your husband going to rock the cradle while you attend board meetings, or are your children going to be raised by strangers? Is that what you *want*?'

'I want what *you* take for granted—the right to choose for myself!' she exclaimed heatedly.

Trent threw up his hands in a mock defensive gesture, and Laurel caught the glint of a fine gold and jet signet ring that matched the cufflinks, and had the initials TFC entwined on it.

'Help! A fully-fledged feminist!' he said wryly.

In some dimly understood recess of her mind, Laurel was aware that this man was deliberately winding her up, and thoroughly enjoying the sport she had provided all too easily for him.

'Don't patronise me, Mr Trent FC whoever-you-are!' she flashed. 'I happen to believe I'm your equal, and that isn't a capital crime—yet!'

His eyes rested thoughtfully on her. She was gamine rather than conventionally pretty, her mouth really too generous for her small face, her eyes too large, the black hair curling naturally under and inwards where it just reached her shoulders, all of which gave her an aura of feyness. But she vibrated energy and determination.

'Only a fool would underrate you on account of your size or your sex, Laurel,' he said, and now his voice was no longer teasing. 'There must be something in the air of this little island that breeds formidable females, from Queen Victoria to Mrs Thatcher. I'd enjoy taking you on in a straight fight. But I'd win, don't ever doubt it.'

Laurel regarded him carefully from beneath lowered dark lashes of incredible length. She was up to here, today, with men intent on putting her down, and for a moment a hot retort hovered on her lips. She bit it back. This man...Trent...she didn't know him at all, and yet she sensed the latent power behind the beautifully tailored suit and the enigmatic smile.

I'd win, don't ever doubt it... For a moment, one treacherous moment, she thought perhaps it would be no shame to capitulate to such an adversary. Then she stamped hard on the thought, for from there it was a short step to taking pleasure in the submission, and Laurel was not by nature a submissive woman.

She was spared the necessity of framing a suitable retort by the arrival of the coffee he had ordered, but while they were drinking it she observed a slight frown crease his forehead, a narrowing of the brows which seemed to indicate that he had something serious on his mind.

'I'm going to hand you some advice, Laurel, which you may or may not like...in fact I think it probable you'll resent it like hell.'

Her eyes smouldered balefully. 'In that case, why bother?'

'Because I think it's appropriate, and the fear of others' opinions has never yet stopped me from acting or speaking as I think fit.' Trent's crisp, decisive tone stopped her protest dead in its tracks, her mouth opened and closed again, and she sat turned to stone, transfixed by his unmistakable authority.

'This...take-over...sale...whatever you choose to call it...don't be pigheaded enough to reject it out of hand. The greater resources of a large organisation could open up new fields of opportunity for your company and those who work for it. Not least yourself, if you're prepared to stand on your own merit, not simply as your father's daughter.'

This was too much! Who did he think he was, dictating to her in this manner?

'Naturally I'd stand on my own merit—if I stayed on with the company,' she flashed. 'Right now, I consider it a sell-out and a betrayal, and I'm not so sure I *want* to work for the new owners, whoever they are.'

He shrugged.

'Have you considered they may not want you—particularly if you take that attitude on board?' he said slyly, and Laurel's head jerked up sharply, her puzzled stare an unintended admission that the thought had not occurred to her.

'Why, that's ridiculous!' she declared indignantly. 'I work very hard, I *know* the business—they'd need me!'

'No one's indispensable,' he observed. Watching her small hands clench in outrage, he continued more calmly, 'Whatever you decide to do, Laurel, make the decision coolly, after consideration—not in an angry huff, as now.' Humour gleamed in the golden irises, and the hollows appeared again in his jaw. 'I hardly know you, but I recognise a powerful temper when I see it. Don't allow it to rule you.'

He was so unerringly apt in his summing up of her present state and her character that she began to chafe with irritation. How could a total stranger understand so much about her after an hour in her company and a brief exchange of words? He had no business to presume, and to hit so near the mark! She was about to tell him roundly what he could do with his advice when the landlord came over to their table.

'Excuse me, sir—miss—but the breakdown people have arrived,' he told them. 'The chap's outside now, and he says he's going to need the lady's car keys.'

Laurel went out to the entrance hall. An icy blast hit her as she opened the door to the two warmly muffled up mechanics, and she surveyed the white wasteland with a shudder.

'Brr!' she exclaimed involuntarily, handing over her keys. 'Hope you can still find the car!'

The elder of the two grinned.

'Don't you worry, miss. We're old hands at this,' he assured her. 'We'll go and get her on the truck. No need for you to come out in the cold—we'll pick you up on the way back.'

Laurel closed the door thankfully behind them and, turning, almost walked into Trent's arms. She had not heard him come up behind her, and her startled heart began to bump irregularly as she looked up into his face.

He gazed down at her quizzically from his lofty height.

'Everything all right?'

'Y . . . yes.' Out here, away from the continuing revelry in the bar, it was very quiet and she felt very much alone with him. Alone and . . . unprotected. It was ridiculous, she told herself. He was not some robber baron about to spirit her away into the night, but a no doubt perfectly respectable businessman with whom she had whiled away an hour.

But it was the other image that persisted, and she knew without being told that he wasn't pleasant and unexceptional. He was fascinating, enigmatic... and possibly dangerous.

'Everything's fine,' she insisted with deliberate and, she hoped, convincing firmness. 'The garage men have gone to get the car, and they'll give me a lift into Lewes. Thank you for... your company. I must pay for my share of the meal.'

'No, you most certainly must not,' he said decidedly. 'That will be my pleasure. If you feel you should thank me... well, it's Christmas, and the facilities are provided.'

Her gaze followed his, upwards to where a bushy sprig of mistletoe hung suspended from the ceiling.

'I think not——' she began indignantly, but before she could take another breath he bent—quite easily for so tall a man—and stopped her mouth with his. It was not the casual kiss acquaintances exchanged ritually under the mistletoe, but a deep, searching, searing statement of possession which took her over, completely and entirely, robbing her of reasonable thought. His hands rested squarely on her shoulders at first, and then, as his mouth deepened its claim on hers, he parted her jacket and cupped the fullness of her breasts.

Her response was instinctive and immediate. Her lips parted, her nipples hardened under his probing fingers expertly seeking their way beneath her blouse to touch her skin. She could feel his impatient desire to remove her clothes, and for a crazy moment her own matched it.

Releasing her mouth, Trent murmured persuasively into her ear, 'You don't *have* to go, Laurel. I have a room booked. This could be quite delightful.'

Her senses returned, and with them her anger, directed now fully against him. So that was his game, was it? Pick up some woman who was in difficulties through no fault of her own, feed her, sympathise with her, exert all his considerable charm and use her to relieve the boredom of the evening!

Well, not this woman! Laurel thought fiercely, jumping back and pulling her jacket together, her eyes snapping with mingled fury and shame. Whatever could she be thinking of, letting herself be groped in a pub entrance hall, as if she were no more than an easy pick-up?

'Not so fast, hot-shot!' she hissed angrily at him. 'I'm not the pushover you seem to think! I might have guessed where that softly-softly approach was leading, but this is as far as it goes!'

Turning her back on him, she marched back into the bar lounge, stalked over to their table, shrugged on her coat and snatched up her handbag. Slamming her way out into the hall, she found him still there, leaning negligently against the stairwell, looking calmly amused and for all the world as if he could not imagine what all the fuss was about.

This nonchalant unconcern only served to make Laurel even more distracted. Rummaging in her bag, she grabbed a couple of five-pound notes and flung them at his feet.

'That's the only way I pay for anything I have!' she declared, and wrenched open the door to the frozen Siberian landscape outside.

Trent made no move to pick up the money, either to pocket it or to return it to her. Head slightly tilted to one side, he regarded her with lazy amusement.

'Baby, it's mighty cold out there,' he intoned softly. Laurel's eyes fixed on him with black fury, and he gave a gentle, regretful shrug. She could not bear to watch again the intriguing crease of his jawline as he smiled, and, shivering at the onslaught of cold wind and sleet, she stomped out into the night, slamming the door behind her.

CHAPTER TWO

CHRISTMAS was not the light-hearted season it usually was in the Ashby household. A certain unavoidable constraint overhung the festivities, and Laurel and her father treated one another with an unaccustomed wary politeness.

Ana, the warm-hearted Spaniard whom Robert had married when Laurel was ten, was palpably unhappy about the unhealed breach. Twelve years her husband's junior, a widow when she married him, although they had known each other much longer, Ana had never had any children of her own, and she had lavished her affections on Laurel, who had never known closeness to another woman until Ana had taken over their household. Now they were more like two widely spaced sisters, or a niece and a favourite aunt, but the closeness was still there, and so was the tie which bound them to one another—their love for the same man, Robert Ashby.

'Laurel, do not be too hard on your father,' Ana had pleaded softly as they trimmed the tree together, a ritual they had always shared.

'*Me*, hard on *him*? Ana, that's a good one!' Laurel answered wryly as she fixed the silver star on the topmost branch. 'After what he's about to do—not only to me, but to everyone else who works for him! You can't expect me to be ecstatic about the prospect.'

'Business I don't understand. Only family,' Ana declared firmly, her way of stating that she had no intention of getting involved in the internecine warfare of

27

office politics. 'It is his decision, and as his daughter you must accept it with grace. Always he has done what is best for you.'

'Not this time. And I don't go along with that philosophy, Ana. It went out with the arranged marriage and the bustle,' argued Laurel. 'What's more, if I *were* his daughter he would have thought twice before taking such action.'

Although it was dark, the velvet curtains at the long windows of the sitting-room were still open to the night, for the spacious split-level house looked out across the Downs, and there was no one to gaze in at the lighted tableau of the room. Laurel stood silhouetted against the window, and the pain in her eyes was more than Ana could bear.

'Oh, no, don't say that! You are—you have always been—his dear child. You might almost have been mine too,' she said, putting her arms round the girl.

Laurel rested her cheek affectionately against her stepmother's for a moment and smiled through the hurt. *That* was certainly true. They were of a height, and although Ana's skin was Mediterranean olive they had the same dark eyes, and Laurel's hair was only a shade lighter. Many, meeting them for the first time, believed them to be truly mother and daughter, and Laurel had often thought it strange that they should be so alike, although unrelated.

'So I believed, until now,' she said soberly, and for the first time in years the thought flickered through her mind—whose daughter am I, really?

When she was a child, Robert had told her only that she was the offspring of a friend who had been unable to keep her. That had satisfied her until her mid-teens, and when she had approached the subject again Ana had been so wounded that she had quickly dropped it and put it from her mind. Whoever her real parents were, they obviously had not wanted her, she reasoned, and while Robert and Ana so patently adored her, that hadn't mattered so much. But now?

She had tried to talk to Robert about his decision to sell Caterplus the night she arrived home after being marooned in the snowbound inn with the mysterious stranger. It had not been a good time to embark on a serious discussion. She was already wound up from the events of the evening, feeling that Trent, who had initially presented himself as a knight on a white charger, had in truth been no more than an opportunist rake, out to take advantage of her.

But her mouth was still bruised by his kiss, her breasts tingled with the memory of his touch, and her body seemed to be crying out for a raw satisfaction she had never felt in need of until now. In this erratic, uncertain frame of mind she had bearded her father in his study.

'I don't understand the necessity to sell,' she had stated. 'After all, the company is doing well.'

Robert Ashby's heavy, broad-shouldered frame was as immovable as the Rock of Gibraltar as he faced her across his desk.

'Tolerably well, although to make the quantum leap into a bigger league it needs an injection of cash I can't raise any other way. We aren't big enough to float shares and go public.' He had frowned, his forehead compressing his thick grey eyebrows. 'Look, Laurel, I can do without this hassle. I'm selling, and that's it.'

'But why?' she persisted. Alarm flared in her eyes as she demanded, 'You aren't ill, are you?'

'Do I have to be? I've worked hard all my life, and I'm tired. I want to rest, spend some time in the sun.

Spend some time with Ana,' he replied testily. 'Is that too much for a man of my years to ask? Damn it, Laurel, most of the money from the sale will come to you— ultimately. And it will make you a fairly wealthy woman. What more do you ask?'

'I don't want the money. I want the company. I've grown up with it, and it's been my life,' Laurel had declared obstinately.

He had placed both hands squarely on the top of his desk, and with a sinking heart she recognised the finality of that gesture. She knew it well enough. It meant—no more. Subject dismissed.

'You've worked hard, done well, and there's no reason why you shouldn't continue to do so,' he said flatly. 'But building up this business has taken the bigger part of my life, and I don't want it to swallow up yours. Have a husband, Laurel, a home and a family. I know what I'm talking about. You—and Ana—came to me late, and I know what I missed, all those years, wrapped up in work. That's why I want out, now.'

Laurel had bent her glossy dark head miserably, recognising the utter implacability of his tone. Still, she had felt impelled to make one last bid.

'What about Clive? Doesn't he have any say in the matter?'

The ghost of a grin twitched Robert's lips.

'Clive? Where the business is concerned, he'd be as much use as a chocolate teapot,' he said baldly. 'You know he's never evinced the slightest interest in it.'

Laurel could not refute this. Clive was Robert's nephew, three years older than Laurel, and he had come to live with them when both his parents died in an accident. He was fun, and he and Laurel had always been friends, but they were chalk and cheese. Since leaving college, where he had just scraped through with a third-class arts degree, Clive had stumbled from one job to another, never really sure of what direction he wanted to take, coasting along on the surface of life, gleaning what he could from it without too much thought for the future. The most he had ever done for his uncle's catering supplies business was to drive one of the delivery vans during his vacation. When they last heard from him, he was minding the country mansion of some wealthy female who was away on the Riviera, although Laurel realised that when he arrived home for Christmas there could well be another story.

Arguing with Robert when he had made up his mind was about as productive as banging one's head against a brick wall, and only slightly less painful. Laurel had stalked out of the study, head high, the light of battle still gleaming in her eyes, but bereft of ammunition to carry on the fight.

She had run the water in the bath, and lain for a long time soaking away the frustrations of the day with perfumed bath oil and steam, and when she'd managed to tear her thoughts away from the impending sale of Caterplus she'd found that they fixed themselves on the image of a man.

A tall, limber man in a fine grey flannel suit, a man with gleaming gold-bronze hair and leonine eyes. The glint of a gold and jet ring, the tiny hollows either side of his mouth when he smiled. The haunting voice, so hard to pin down, the warm, all too knowing hands caressing her...

Laurel had submerged herself in the soapy water, trying to drown out the little prickles of sensation creeping over her skin.

'You really don't have to go...this could be quite delightful...'

Even now, feeling as she did that the mysterious Trent had been out to make use of her, she did not doubt that it could indeed have been so. Something inside her wished that she had stayed at the inn, gone with him to his room and let him make love to her. And that was disturbing, because she had never had wanton thoughts like that before.

It must be simply the end result of the way I'm feeling, the disruption in my life, she told herself, stepping resolutely out of the tub and wrapping herself in a vast, fluffy bathtowel. I'm the last person to allow myself to be seduced by a practised charmer like that. Which is the best I can say for him.

Then she recalled the dryness of his voice and the guarded emptiness lurking behind the tawny eyes as he surveyed the merrymakers. A man far from home—wherever that was—alone and with only business to occupy his time. Ships that pass in the night. A hand closing steadyingly over hers—the loneliness of one human being reaching out towards the distress of another.

Was he, for some unknown reason, as unhappy as she? And if so, what might that reason be?

I'll never know, Laurel had thought as she shrugged on her satin nightdress. And somehow that had only served to increase the desolation in her heart.

Clive arrived home on Christmas Eve, laden with presents and bonhomie.

'Phew!' he exclaimed, tossing back his thick chestnut mane that looked, as always, in need of a cut. 'The cop cars are out in force tonight! I stopped to have a few drinks with some old mates in the White Hart, and I was lucky to dodge the boys in blue on the way home.'

'You shouldn't drink and drive,' Laurel said censoriously, trying to suppress the twinkle in her eye. 'It's irresponsible, and besides, we don't want to lose you.'

'*Dios*, no!' echoed Ana. 'You are a very naughty boy, Clive, always have been. Now you must promise not to go out again before I pour you this drink, or you get only Coca-Cola.'

He crossed the fingers of both hands.

'Scout's honour! I've just driven down from Northumbria, and I ain't goin' no place. Besides, you're cooking paella, unless my sense of smell has deserted me. Where's the old man?'

Ana too was trying hard not to smile.

'Your uncle, if that's who you mean, will be down in a moment. He's...he's changing,' she said.

'Lawks, we haven't started dressing for dinner, have we?' exclaimed Clive, alarmed. 'Do I have to nip down to Moss Bros for a DJ?'

'*Sit!*' ordered Ana, pushing him into a chair, and Laurel said,

'Father was just out walking the dogs. I expect he got muddy and needed to freshen up.'

Robert had taken to spending a lot of time cloistered in his study, or up in his and Ana's bedroom, and Laurel could only conclude that it was the atmosphere between the two of them which made him keep absenting himself. She had tried her best—after all, it *was* Christmas—but she had been unable to keep her darker feelings entirely under wraps. These last few minutes since Clive turned up had been the lightest the household had known for some time.

They were still laughing, Laurel fixing drinks, and Ana handing round *tapas*—little snacks of olives, seafood and savouries, a custom she had brought with her from Spain—when Robert walked in, and immediately a cloud darkened the room. It was nothing specific that either he or Laurel did, it was just there, whenever he and she were present together. Robert *did* look tired and strained, Laurel thought, and briefly her conscience smote her. Then her rebellious heart fought back—there was no need for this estrangement. He himself had brought it on them.

Later that evening, when Robert and Ana had retired to bed, Laurel curled up in a corner of the sofa and Clive sprawled on the rug in front of the dying embers of the fire while he told her of the collapse of his latest employment venture.

'The old bat came back from the Côte d'Azur for Christmas, would you believe, with a load of house guests, and inveigled her old butler out of retirement to run the show for her,' he said glumly. 'Consequently, she doesn't need me any more, so I'm back on the dole queue. I didn't like to mention it at dinner—the atmosphere was loaded enough. What the hell is going on here?'

Laurel told him, but while his reaction to her distress was sympathetic he did not share either her surprise or her outrage.

'I suppose the old boy's entitled to a rest, if that's what he wants, and he can well afford to retire,' he said with a shrug. 'If he can get a good price for the company, why not?'

'And what about me, Clive? My future? Doesn't that count for anything?' she demanded.

'Your future, my girl, will be spent keeping some lucky bloke's bed warm,' he grinned irreverently.

Laurel uncurled herself and jumped up, shaking with indignation. Her father, and Clive, and the stranger she had met in the pub, for all he had qualified his response, had all expressed roughly similar opinions. Anyone might think the twentieth century hadn't dawned, and that generations of women hadn't fought hard for their place in it.

'What does a woman have to do to get herself taken seriously around here?' she demanded disgustedly. 'I'm going to bed!'

Somehow they got through Christmas. The turkey and plum pudding, the carol-singing and present-giving, all the traditional things went on as if everything were the same, although Laurel found it hard to maintain the pretence. Unwrapping the diamond and amethyst pendant Robert had given her, she found herself wondering briefly about Trent, and where he had spent the festive season.

Was there a woman somewhere saying, 'Thank you, darling,' while his golden eyes rested tenderly on her? A woman who was unaware that he had an unfortunate tendency to pick up unattached girls in pubs and try to seduce them into his bed? Or was he alone somewhere, pretending the jollity and conviviality were not happening?

On New Year's Eve Clive and Laurel were invited to a dance at the Rugby Club, of which he was still nom- inally a member, while Robert and Ana were celebrating the occasion more sedately, having dinner with friends.

'Let's whizz up to the Golf Club first,' said Clive, who was still in the process of catching up with old friends. 'We can take my car and go on to the dance in it, then we can always walk home afterwards, when we're sure to have imbibed a good deal.'

'All right,' said Laurel, who had already taken the precaution of booking a taxi for the homeward journey. She didn't trust Clive to stick to his determination not to drink and drive.

She was wearing a long dress of fuchsia-coloured crêpe-de-Chine with a halter neckline that bared most of her back and plunged to a deep V at the front. Of necessity, she was braless, but her breasts were high and firm and her cleavage could stand the exposure. Robert's pendant sparkled at her throat, and in her dark hair she wore a single silk flower to match her dress.

'Qué linda!' Ana clapped her hands appreciatively. 'You will catch all eyes in that, *cariña*! Wear your shawl, and make sure you don't also catch cold.'

Laurel picked up the lacy black Spanish mantilla Ana had given her, and Clive draped it round her shoulders.

'What d'you reckon, Uncle Robert? Dare I be seen with this siren?' he grinned. 'Little Laurel sure has grown up!'

Robert frowned, something like regret showing in his eyes as he surveyed Laurel's womanly curves and sleek, upswept hairstyle.

'Too damn much, and too damn soon,' he growled. 'See you look after her!'

For all there was concerned and caring affection in her father's eyes, Laurel could not suppress a rising annoyance as she accompanied Clive out of the house. Look after her, indeed! She was twenty-one, Lewes was a small town, and she had lived there all her life! She could perfectly well look after herself, and she was only going to a New Year's Eve hop, not a Bacchanalian orgy. Why did everyone imagine that because one was five feet three and female one was in need of protection? As she eased herself into the front seat of the MG Robert had given Clive on his twenty-first birthday she thought, I'm not going to enjoy tonight. She couldn't will herself into the spirit of it. It would have been as well to stay in her room and read a book.

But Clive was in fine form, and ready to enter enthusiastically into the revels. *He* wasn't worrying about the future, for all he was presently out of a job, she realised, and instead of raising her spirits his insouciance only irritated her. Gritting her teeth, she forced a smile to her face as the car wound up the steep hill towards the Golf Club.

The snow which had caused her problems a few days earlier had been only a temporary phenomenon, and now the usual mild, benevolent Yuletide weather of southern England had reasserted itself. The Golf Club perched high on the cliffs above the Cuilfail Tunnel, and from the windows of its bar lounge, looked out over a splendid panorama of Lewes spread out below it, the steep, narrow streets leading up to the castle ruins, and the long high street easy to pick out.

To her further annoyance, having put a glass of gin and tonic in her hand, Clive proceeded to abandon her as he made the rounds of several ex-cronies he recognised. For a while Laurel chatted desultorily to a couple of Robert's friends, but not being a regular golfer she knew no one present very closely, and resorted to gazing out of the window, wishing they could leave. It really wasn't very thoughtful of Clive.

And then, turning to seek him out in the throng and send him a silent message that she had had enough, she found herself looking clear across the room into the eyes of the Renaissance prince! For several moments they stared at one another with the shock of recognition which always came on finding someone in a place where one had not expected them to be. And then she was conscious that she was no longer bored, that the evening she had wished over had suddenly lifted itself on to another plane, and the air around her quivered with expectancy and excitement. His deep-set tawny eyes held hers briefly, and then she turned away, confused and all of a shiver, deliberately resuming her study of the town below.

He did not seek her out immediately. She stood for a full five minutes with her back to him, consciously waiting for him to do so, although she tried to convince herself she was doing no such thing. Then she felt a light touch on her bare shoulder.

'Hello again, Laurel. That's a stunning dress you're almost wearing.'

She turned, looking up into his faintly smiling face. Tonight he wore a dark lounge suit which accentuated the bright gold of his shining hair. His expression did not alter as his glance flickered over her, but she could have sworn he was reminding her that he knew very well what it felt like to touch her.

'I'm going on to a dance. In the circumstances, a glimpse of flesh shouldn't shock anyone,' she said coolly. 'I'm surprised to find you still around here. Didn't you go home for Christmas?'

'Ah, you're assuming I didn't, but you don't know where "home" is for me, do you?' he said obliquely, true to form giving nothing away. 'Did you manage to get your car fixed?'

'It had to have a new battery. Not that the other one was all that old, but these things happen,' she replied, trying hard to think as she talked. What was he doing here? She was fairly sure he wasn't local; they would have met, and she would certainly have remembered him. But one had to be a member or a member's guest to be at the Golf Club. He had to be visiting someone, and although he had intimated that he was on business, he could have stayed over for Christmas. Which would seem to bear out that his home base was too far away for a short trip back. 'I didn't expect to run into you tonight.'

'No? But then life's full of surprises. It prevents our becoming too complacent,' he smiled. 'Don't tell me you're unescorted again, Laurel? Is it a penchant of yours?'

'It is when I'm on business,' she retorted crossly. 'Not on social occasions. Of course I'm with someone. And you?'

'Oh, I'm with...several people,' he agreed, which told her very little, as she was sure he fully intended. But the fact that he was here meant that someone knew him, and given that, it might take her a while, but it was surely not beyond her to find out what he seemed to delight in not telling her.

Over the heads of several people, she caught sight of Clive waving to her. Damn! Trust him to want to leave now, just when she had her mind set on a little detective work! Could he be put off for a while?

'I think someone's trying to attract your attention,' Trent said softly, his smile deepening as he sensed her frustration. 'You mustn't keep him waiting. Happy New Year, Laurel. It's a little early, so we'll take the customary kiss as having already been given!'

She scowled.

'There's no way you could persuade me to repeat it!' she declared stiffly, and the fine eyebrows drew thoughtfully together.

'Oh, I don't know. "Had we but world enough and time—this coyness, lady, were no crime",' he said with quiet flippancy.

'Well, we haven't. We never could have,' she said flatly, aware that she was lying, and aware that he knew she was lying. Even while he annoyed her intensely and aroused an instinctive antagonism in her, she had a strange·hankering to feel his mouth on hers once more.

'Laurel! Come on!' Clive called to her across the room.

'Your swain is getting impatient,' Trent observed amusedly. 'I hope you can keep him confined within the bounds of propriety, although wearing a dress like that it won't be easy.'

'What makes you think I want to? Perhaps it's only over-sexed Casanovas in pubs I like to keep in their place!' she riposted with satisfaction, and, turning her back on him, she stalked over to where Clive was waiting.

Why should she have told him that her escort tonight was the boy she had grown up with, and not a prospective or actual lover? It was none of his business, and she was quite happy for him to get the wrong impression. Let him think that she had someone in her life with whom she would gladly do all she had refused to do with him! He behaved as if he fully expected to get his way with any female he fancied—let him think that he turned her right off!

But deep inside her a persistent voice told her that he was convinced less by her words than by the secret language of her body, which it was far less easy to control.

'Who's that you were talking to?' Clive asked curiously as they walked out to the car park.

'I don't know. I saw him in a pub the other day, but I haven't a clue who he is,' she replied. 'I was hoping you'd be able to tell me what he's doing here at the Golf Club.'

'I've never seen him before in my life,' Clive admitted, 'but he was looking at you as though he'd have liked to devour you. Don't fancy him, do you?'

'Certainly not!' Laurel said emphatically. Not even to Clive, whom she had known for years, was she going to admit to a perverse attraction to this annoying stranger.

It was late when they arrived home that night, and the house was in silence. Laurel's feet ached in her three-inch-heeled silver sandals. She had thrown herself into the gaiety of the evening with feverish energy, danced every dance, drunk enough to make her feel pleasantly cheerful, given out a lot of perfunctory pecks under the mistletoe and good-naturedly fended off any more enthusiastic embraces.

'I'm for bed!' she exclaimed exhaustedly, turning her key in the lock and kicking off her shoes in the hall, wriggling her toes gratefully in the deep pile of the Berber carpet. 'That was fun, Clive. Thanks for a great evening. Oh... and Happy New Year.'

'Don't I get a kiss, then? All the other chaps got one,' said Clive aggrievedly, sounding so much like a little boy who'd been refused a biscuit that Laurel giggled.

'Oh, sure...I'm sorry,' she laughed, standing on tiptoe to kiss his cheek.

To her amazement he grabbed hold of her and pulled her to him, hard.

'I didn't mean like that!' he said thickly. 'I meant a proper kiss, Laurel—like this!'

His mouth came down on hers, wet and eager, his hands clamped over her buttocks and then groped their way up her body, making her squirm with displeasure. She pulled away firmly, breathing heavily and glaring at him with angry distress.

'Clive, stop it! You've had too much to drink!' she said sharply. 'It's me, Laurel—remember? Why, I'm practically your sister!'

'But you *aren't* my sister,' he said sullenly. 'You aren't even my cousin—not that it would matter if we were cousins. As it happens, we aren't actually related by blood at all.'

'No...but that's the way I think about you!' she cried. 'We grew up together. We're friends. Don't spoil that!'

'The way you look now, Laurel, few men would be content just to be your friend,' he said darkly. 'I saw the way you were giving *him* the come on—that man at the Golf Club. Just about begging him for it! So if it could be him, why not me?'

She stared at him, eyes dark with humiliation, as the last of her safe, innocent youth ebbed away, the final bastion of home fell to alien, unknown forces.

'You're mistaken. I don't know that man from Adam, and I won't be seeing him again,' she said firmly. 'I'm going to bed now, Clive. Goodnight.'

Happy New Year, Laurel, she said wretchedly to herself as she trailed upstairs to her room. From now on, nothing was ever going to be the same again.

CHAPTER THREE

PART OF Laurel was glad to get back to work after the break, but part of her dreaded it. Heavy on her lay the burden of what she knew, and no one else, as yet, did, although according to Robert certain members of the management team would be less surprised than she.

'And less bolshie about it,' he muttered sourly, at which Laurel had flashed him a furious stare.

'Well, perhaps. *They'll* only be working for a new employer. They won't have been effectively disinherited,' she snapped back at him.

'Don't be ridiculous,' Robert said scathingly. 'Who's going to inherit the money from the sale—along with the rest of my estate, eventually? *You* are, madam, so stop inventing a drama where none exists. Most young women would swoon with delight at the notion.'

He had explained carefully to his family that a sizeable sum of money would go immediately into trust for Laurel, to be hers when she married or reached the age of twenty-five, whichever came first. The remainder of his estate was willed to Ana, and, through her, to Laurel. There was also a certain provision for Clive.

'Although considerably smaller, because you have already inherited what your father left you, and you'll have to wait for my demise before you get anything from me,' he had explained to his nephew.

'In other words, he's not giving me anything right now to fritter away on another of my harebrained schemes,' Clive had said gloomily to Laurel when they were alone.

'The message is, "knuckle down and make your way, lad, as I did at your age."'

'He has a point,' she remarked, not without a certain smug satisfaction. He had not been altogether sympathetic about Robert's plans for *her*. 'You *are* wasting your abilities, Clive, and sooner or later you'll have to stop mucking about.' She poured water into the teapot and topped up both their cups. 'He's tied my hands too, you know. I can't take my share of the money from the sale and set up my own operation, as I'd like to do. I have to wait until I'm twenty-five, four whole years away!'

'Or get married,' he reminded her.

'That's not even a possibility,' she said firmly. 'I'm not that heavily involved with anyone, nor do I intend to be.'

'OK, you can lay off the hints,' he grinned, but Laurel did not share his smile. Things had been different between them since New Year's Eve, and she thought it would take time to recapture their easy, casual friendship—if indeed they could ever go back to it. Although he had rather sheepishly apologised to her for his behaviour the next day.

'You were right—I'd had a skinful, although I was by no means drunk,' he had defended himself. 'It was just that you looked so bloody enticing in that dress, I got a bit carried away. I didn't mean to come on so strong.'

Laurel had been a mite doubtful about this explanation. It seemed to her that he was apologising only for rushing his fences, not for the fact that he had made a pass at her at all. As if, had he only taken it more gently, she might have responded to his attentions. It wasn't the case. Laurel thought of him as something between a brother and a friend, and knew she could never think of him any other way. She thought he should realise that, and she had never expected him to feel differently about her. Still, she had accepted his apology at its face value, and told him it would be best if they forgot the incident had ever happened.

He was sprawled on the couch reading a newspaper when she left for work the first day back after the holiday.

'My word, we're into power dressing these days, aren't we?' he jibed.

Laurel was wearing a pure wool skirt and long-line jacket in discreet grey Prince of Wales check, with a tailored white blouse beneath it. Her dark bob of hair was pinned back neatly behind her ears, and her small feet were encased in soft grey leather high-heeled boots.

'We can't all lie around all day in scruffy jeans and a sweater, just waiting for the pubs to open,' she retorted pithily.

'I'll have you know I'm working hard. Studying form,' he said, and she noted that the paper was open at the racing column. 'There's a meeting at Plumpton. I might just toddle along there later. When I've fathomed out what's going to win.'

Laurel shook her head as she hurried out to her car. Clive was incorrigible, but she worried about him. He couldn't go on like this forever.

However, she could not dwell on his problems for too long. She had plenty of her own today.

Robert Ashby had started his company from a small, rented premises comprising a kitchen and an office. From there, in the early days, he had supplied the neighbouring offices and small firms of the town with sandwiches and hot soup at lunchtime. Business had boomed, and his creation expanded, until now he had a fine, purpose-built block on the outskirts of Lewes, and the sandwich take-away was now only a small part of the operation.

Gleaming kitchens under the expert supervision of a qualified chef had dreamed up a range of ready-to-serve frozen dishes to which new additions were continually being added, and these were whisked all over the county to pubs, restaurants and staff cafeterias in the blue and white Caterplus refrigerated vans. There was also a gourmet section which cooked and served dinner parties in people's homes or executive dining-rooms, and could call on the services of a list of skilled personnel when required.

Food had fascinated Robert Ashby from an early age, but he had not been content simply to open a restaurant and cater only for the select few. He had wanted to bring good quality, interesting eating to the many in the course of their daily lives, and had had the imaginative vision to see how it might be achieved.

Laurel had a lump in her throat as she put her car in the car park and pushed open the double glass doors to the pleasantly impressive reception with its leather banquette seats, glossy pot-plants, and the long teak desk behind which Sarah, the receptionist, presided over the telephone and dealt with personal callers.

'Good morning, Sarah. Nice holiday?'

The receptionist raised her eyes to the ceiling with a smile.

'Not bad. It's good to get the kids off back to school and get back to normal once more. How was your Christmas?'

Laurel grinned.

'Pretty much like everyone's, I suppose. Too much eating, drinking, and general over-indulgence.'

Was she being evasive? She couldn't say more at this stage about what lay ahead, and if she did warn people, what purpose would it serve? Passing through the accounts section, she paused to chat with Alan, the chief accountant, and Janet, his assistant. Janet was a widow with two sons at college. She needed her job. Laurel frowned. There were plenty like her, who could do without the uncertainty of a management upheaval.

She sniffed the air appreciatively. Something interesting was happening in the kitchen, and she couldn't resist popping her head round the door to investigate.

'Hi, Robin. That smells fantastic!'

Robin glanced up absently from whatever he was stirring, his small, alert eyes gleaming with the zeal of discovery under his high chef's hat.

'Hello, Laurel. It's one of the new range—Chicken Tikka. Still experimental, but should be ready for testing soon. Want to try it out at lunchtime?'

'Mm—love to. If I can wait that long.'

Laurel left him busily stirring, adding and tasting, and went to her own small office. The cleaners had been in, and there wasn't a speck of dust, but it had that musty smell after being shut up for a fortnight. Laurel opened the window a little, watered her plants, and sat down at her desk to open her mail. A lot of it was junk which had accumulated over the holidays, and as she skimmed through it and tossed it into the wastepaper basket her mind went wandering back over the years.

As a small girl, she'd gone along with Robert to the 'shop', begging to be allowed to butter and fill the sandwich rolls. Later, in her school holidays, she had worked in the kitchens, in the office, and as soon as she passed her driving test she had been out on the vans. Robert had fostered and encouraged her interest, gratified that the child he had adopted should want to follow him into the company, and after she had taken a year's business studies course at Brighton Polytechnic Laurel had been back at Caterplus in earnest, learning her way through every department. In spite of her youth, no one doubted that she had earned her place. And this was her reward, she mused ruefully.

The summons came halfway through the morning. In terms of manpower, Caterplus was still a relatively small, streamlined operation, and it was possible for all the staff to gather in the small canteen-rest-room area. It wasn't unheard-of for Robert to gather the entire workforce together when he had something of importance to say—he knew everyone by name, and preferred to communicate face to face, rather than via the impersonality of the memo pad. And how long would that happy state of affairs last? Laurel wondered, as she perched on the edge of a table, looking around her at faces which were interested, but not unduly troubled.

She watched those expressions alter as her father talked.

'There's only one way to tell people something important which affects them, and that's straight out. So I'll come to the point. I'm retiring and selling the company,' he said, without preamble.

There were several gasps, and quite a few frowns. People on the whole mistrusted change and felt it boded ill for them. But Laurel observed that Alan, for one, did not look as if stricken by a bolt from the blue, and she sensed his accountant's brain ticking away, keeping pace with Robert's words.

There were questions, of course, which he invited and declared himself prepared to answer.

'Can you tell us how soon this...changeover...will come into effect?' Robin wanted to know.

'Not precisely, but I envisage very soon. As a matter of fact, I have a potential buyer making serious enquiries, right now.'

Laurel's dark head jerked up. He had never told her that, far from simply deciding to sell, he had quietly put matters in motion, and already someone...anonymous and threatening...was sniffing at the bait. She gazed at him almost accusingly as he went on.

'Since I have every reason to believe the sale will go through, I am able to tell you that in the very near future you will all be working for Castleford Industries. I expect the name will be familiar to you.'

A buzz of excited conversation spread around the room. There could be few who had not heard of this multi-national corporation, one of the most powerful modern business empires, American-based, with headquarters in Boston, Massachusetts. But Laurel was still silent. Her worst fears had just been realised. Castleford Industries would swallow up Caterplus whole, without noticing. As an independent company, it would cease to exist. As individuals, they would all cease to exist. What could her father be thinking of? Couldn't he at least wait until a more sympathetic, more compatible buyer came along?

It was Janet who spoke, voicing what was the deepest fear of most people in the room.

'Mr Ashby, what's going to happen to all of us? When this organisation takes over, will we all still have jobs?'

Robert smiled a little wearily.

'As far as I'm able, Janet, I've ensured that you will. There'll be no initial redundancies. But you will all have to maintain your positions on your own merit, by working as well and as loyally for the new management as you've always done for me.'

He lifted his head and looked across to where his daughter had been sitting, to reinforce the point especially to her. But Laurel had already stood up and walked out of the room.

The sitting-room was awash with travel brochures, and Ana, festooned with carrier bags, had obviously been shopping for new clothes.

'Tea!' she gasped, falling into an armchair. 'My poor feet, they will never recover!'

'I bet the shop assistants at Next are saying the same thing,' said Laurel, getting up and going into the kitchen to put the kettle on. 'Where are you going, anyhow? Is it decided?' she asked when she came back with the tray.

Ana massaged her aching feet.

'The Caribbean. We fly to Miami and then take a cruise ship,' she said.

'Very nice.' Laurel's voice was tight and controlled. Her stepmother gave a shrug.

'It is all your father's idea. I would be quite happy to stay here and relax with him, or go to see my family in Spain,' she said. 'But he seems to want this trip. I think he needs it, Laurel.'

'Oh, don't get me wrong, I think an extended holiday is a great idea, for both of you,' Laurel insisted. 'Only this seems so final—selling up, retiring. Apart from anything else, it's so unlike my father. My own feelings set aside, I wonder if he won't regret it.'

Ana said, 'He is very sure, so I don't question. I want only what he wants. When you love a man—well, *cariña*, you will know, some day.'

Laurel wasn't sure that she ever wanted to love anyone that deeply, or whether she were in fact capable of it. Ana was devoted and loving and sweet. Me? Basically, I'm selfish, perhaps, she thought soberly. I want only what he wants? She doubted there was anyone who could make her feel that way.

'That's not for me. I'm a career girl,' she said. 'Or at least, I *was*.'

'Then you still are,' Robert's voice said crisply from the doorway. 'Castleford is a big corporation, full of opportunities for the young and energetic. Stop feeling sorry for yourself. Get in there and carve yourself a niche. I've written your first year's contract into the agreement. The rest is up to you—if you still want it by then.'

There was war in Laurel's dark eyes.

'Why shouldn't I want it? I'd rather have my money now, and set up in competition. At least half the key staff would come with me,' she declared combatively.

Robert glanced at the tea-tray, changed his mind and poured himself a Scotch.

'And Castleford would annihilate you and put them all out of jobs,' he said testily. 'Grow up, Laurel. You aren't ready for that kind of power yet, and I'm not throwing away a lifetime's work to satisfy girlish pique.'

Laurel was on her feet, trembling with anger, and Ana intervened quickly.

'Please—*por favor*—both of you! Keep all this for the office. I refuse to live on a battleground!' she said firmly but placatingly, and out of love and respect for her, the antagonists both backed off. A faint grin flitted across Robert's tired features.

'I didn't tell the new managing director what a determined, obstinate article you could be,' he said. 'I decided to let him find that out for himself. He'll be coming into the office tomorrow, so you can confirm for yourself that he doesn't have two horns and a tail. But just remember that he's one of Castleford's directors, and from five o'clock tomorrow afternoon he'll be your boss.'

Laurel did not wait around to hear any more about this personage. She still felt deeply betrayed, and had not forgiven her father, but she was very thoughtful as she went up to her room.

She had been involved with Caterplus too long and too thoroughly to want to leave it now, whatever she might say out of hurt or anger. But it could easily prove that the new managing director might not want her, his predecessor's daughter. He was a new broom, and she might well be one of the cobwebs he would sweep out.

Well, she had a year. She would use it to fight for the company's interests as best she could, to ensure that as many staff as possible survived the take-over, try to maintain the happy working atmosphere they were all used to. After that... who knew?

The next morning, Laurel put on her Prince of Wales check suit, which was one of her favourite outfits for work, but with it she wore a bright red silk blouse. She wasn't sure if this could be taken as a statement of rebellion, or if it meant only, 'Here I am—you can't overlook me.' But certainly she felt better sporting this bright banner.

'Today's the day,' Sarah greeted her as she entered, her cheerful manner covering an inner nervousness, Laurel was well aware.

'There's no need for you to worry, Sarah,' she said impulsively. 'You're great at your job. There's no one

stays as unflappable as you do, under pressure.
Castleford will need you out here on the front line.'

Sarah smiled, straightening her shoulders.

'Most of us feel it will be all right so long as *you* stay,
Laurel,' she confided. 'You and Robin and Alan—the
Team. Then we'll still be Caterplus.'

'I'm not planning on going anywhere right now,'
Laurel promised. 'Not without a push.' Infused with the
confidence imparted by the trust of others, she almost
ran lightly up the stairs to her office.

Someone was there before her. A man was sitting at
her desk, using her computer terminal. He wore a well-
cut navy pinstripe suit, with a shirt of palest blue and a
dove-grey silk tie, all of instantly recognisable quality.
His gleaming head was bent over the keyboard into which
he was tapping a message, and against the healthy, tanned
skin of his hands, the gold and black signet ring flashed
as his fingers moved swiftly.

Laurel closed the door behind her and leaned weakly
against it. She uttered one word.

'You!'

The smile on his face as he looked up at her was not
especially welcoming. The intriguing eyes were blank of
all warmth of expression, cool, businesslike.

'How do you do, Miss Ashby,' he said formally. 'I'm
Trenton Foxley-Castleford. I'm sure we shall work well
together.'

A whole host of thoughts rushed headlong through
Laurel's mind as she stared at the man seated behind
her desk. She remembered the snowbound inn, and his
hand steadying her as she seemed about to collapse. She
remembered how she had blurted out the details of the
company's sale, and her own hostility towards it, be-

lieving it hardly mattered, because he was just a stranger passing through, whom she would never see again.

Then she remembered that deeply demanding kiss in the hallway, and the short encounter at the Golf Club, when she had attempted to convince him that she did not find him attractive. A succession of mortifying experiences which she would have been glad to forget, whoever he was. But he wasn't just an annoying, intriguing stranger any more. She was going to have to come in here every day and work under his command. If she had thought, this morning, that her existence had plunged to its nadir, and things could hardly be worse, how very, very mistaken she had been.

'You knew,' she said flatly, accusingly. 'Didn't you? All the time I was telling you my troubles in the pub, you knew you were going to take over the company, and you never said a word—you just let me rabbit on!'

He said calmly, 'It seemed to me that you needed to rabbit on, as you put it. If you hadn't let off some steam when you did, you'd have blown a gasket. And I could hardly not know, could I, when you mentioned your father's company by name?'

'Then why didn't you tell me? Why didn't you stop the charade right there?' she cried, unable, now, to prevent the bitterness pouring out.

'What was I supposed to do? Stand up and announce that I was the ogre about to blight your life?' Trent demanded amusedly. 'You might have hit me over the head with a bottle, the mood you were in!'

His manner changed abruptly, the humour drained away and he became crisp and purposeful.

He said, 'This is getting us nowhere fast, so let's have it out of the way, once and for all. I had a brief of several possible companies to consider, this being one of them.

But nothing was decided, and, having a name that's fairly well known in business circles, I wasn't inclined to broadcast it to possible competitors that I was even in the area.'

'Hence the secrecy,' Laurel said drily.

'Let's call it anonymity,' he suggested coolly.

'You can call it what you like. It stinks of deception to me!' she exclaimed.

Trent rose unhurriedly. She had not forgotten how tall he was, and if she thought sitting behind her desk gave him an in-built advantage, towering over her handed him game, set and match.

'Business is like that, Laurel. You may be a big fish in a small pond here, but you've a lot to learn if you are to survive out in the open sea, where the sharks swim,' he said briskly. 'Now look. Your father speaks highly of your ability, energy and value to the company, but I haven't taken his word for it. I've asked around and had that opinion confirmed.'

Amazed dark pools, her eyes gazed up into his.

'You've what?'

'Naturally. I always investigate all key executives *before* I OK their contracts,' he said. 'The point is this. There's a place for you with Castleford, and you're welcome aboard. But I expect your loyalty and co-operation.'

'You mean I'm not allowed to disagree with you?' she asked sharply.

'On the contrary. I expect you to, if you think you're right, and can make a case for it. What I don't expect you to do is to try to subvert or undermine my authority, in short, to go against me simply for the sake of it. You may think you're safe to play whatever game you like, because you have a year's guaranteed contract, but you give me trouble, lady, and I'll make you only too damn pleased to get out of here, any way. Is that clear?'

'As crystal,' said Laurel, tight-lipped. His voice was hard and brusque, and she was quite sure he meant every word he said. This was no charming rake. This was a corporate piranha! 'You can be assured that I shall do nothing that isn't for the good of this company,' she added, emphasising the last two words very slightly. 'Can you tell me how long you'll be requiring my office? I do have rather a lot of work to do.'

Trent smiled mirthlessly.

'It's all yours, as of this minute,' he said, standing aside to let her get to her seat. Laurel was obliged to brush past him, and she felt every hair follicle on her scalp, every nerve-ending of her skin bristling with awareness of him as they almost but not quite touched. Then he was gone, and she sank into her chair, hands shaking, asking herself how this situation could ever be more than intolerable.

Her eyes strayed absently to her desk, where a crisp new ten-pound note had been left in front of her VDU unit, and she sat bolt upright, transfixed, as she read the lines he had left displayed on the screen.

The grave's a fine and private place
But none I think do there embrace.

The ten pounds repaid the money flung at him in the inn doorway. The couplet, Laurel knew, came from the same poem as the lines he had tossed at her at the Golf Club, and they nagged her all morning until she was obliged to seek them out in her dictionary of quotations, and discover they had been written by a seventeenth-century poet, Andrew Marvell.

A scholar as well as a businessman, Laurel thought grimly; that's all I need. She bent her head over her work, trying to concentrate on some letters to suppliers she was writing, but he would keep on intruding between her and what she was doing.

Would the day ever come when she would get used to working for him? One thing she knew—he would be watching for her, and she had better take care not to trip up or step out of line. He knew exactly how she felt about the new set-up, and he wouldn't be inclined to give her more than one chance.

Some time later her father looked in on her. He had never been given to casual chats in office hours. If he needed to see her, he sent for her, and as a rule he was up to his elbows in work, and kept the meetings brief. But now he looked somehow lost, not quite sure what he was supposed to be doing.

'Now that the hour had come, it's very strange,' he confessed. 'I feel like a spare part.'

Laurel squashed a fleeting sympathy for his plight, which, she thought firmly, he had brought upon himself.

'I knew you'd hate it when it came to actually stepping down,' she said. 'Well, it's what *you* wanted.'

'You don't understand. It *is* what I want,' he insisted. 'It's just the actual process of detaching myself from something which has been part of me for so long which is difficult. Maybe I'll just slip away while no one is looking.'

'Don't you dare!' she ordered warningly. 'There's to be a little farewell ceremony in the canteen this afternoon. You'd better be there, whether you like it or not, and act surprised!'

'I see the new, abrasive management style has already begun to rub off on you,' he murmured. 'I take it Mr Castleford has made himself known?'

'He has,' she said shortly. It did not appear that Trent had mentioned his earlier meetings with her, and for that Laurel supposed she ought to be grateful. 'I know you told me that the new MD was one of Castleford's directors, but he bears the name of the organisation. Surely he's not the founder? I should have thought him too young.'

'And you'd be right. The man who created the Castleford empire is his father, J.J. Castleford, who, so I understand, left his native Liverpool some forty years ago, with a few quid in his wallet and a second-class ticket to America.' He smiled quietly down at her. 'That, Laurel, is a success story which puts mine in its proper perspective.'

'I think you're one hell of a success. I always have thought so,' she said, with a rush of loyalty and affection. It was no good—whatever he had done and however much she disagreed with it, she still loved him.

He inclined his head.

'Perhaps. But it's time for the next chapter, and I can't write it, Laurel. I want to see the company I created move on to bigger things. Like a child, one can't hold it back. And for that it needs money, resources and energy I don't have.'

Laurel watched him go, sadly, and her frighteningly erratic state of mind veered back towards resentment again. Trent Castleford's father hadn't sold out to a stranger and left his son to make his own way. He had made him a director, given him power and responsibility within his organisation. Why did it have to be so easy for him, and so hard for her?

And why, if he were his father's golden boy, had she sensed that air of aloof loneliness, of alienation about him, at their first meeting?

She did not see Trent again until she was just about to go to the farewell ceremony which had been planned for Robert Ashby, when, hurrying along the corridor, she almost collided with him full tilt.

'I know it's Friday afternoon, but can't you wait to get out?' he drawled softly.

Laurel bridled.

'I'm not going home—not right away. We're giving a small party for my father. Drinks, canapés, speeches— that sort of thing.' She hesitated before adding sweetly, 'Why don't you come along?' Let him see the affection and respect everyone felt for Robert, let him know just what he had to live up to, walking in here with his father's name and simply picking up what another man had worked all his life to create!

But Trent shook his head gently.

'I think not,' he said. 'That event is for your father, and it isn't my place to usurp it. I've spent today talking to key members of personnel, but my reign doesn't really commence until Monday. I'll talk to all the staff then. You can set it up for me,' he finished airily.

Laurel drew herself up as tall as she could, which wasn't easy.

'Gloria—my father's secretary—will do that for you,' she said stiffly. 'I'll have a word with her, if you like.'

'Laurel, I don't give a damn who does it, so long as it's done,' he informed her acerbically. 'I haven't worked in Europe for some years, but one hears of a peculiarly English disease which insists on one man for one job— demarcation disputes. I won't have any of that nonsense. Flexibility has to be the keyword.'

'Great—you want *me* to invent and test new recipes, while Robin types your letters, perhaps?' she said sarcastically. 'That should work a treat!'

He looked down on her with amused scorn.

'It's so patently obvious that there are areas where specialisation is necessary, and others where it's not, that I should hardly need to point it out to you,' he replied witheringly. He cast a quick, impatient glance at the gold watch on his wrist. 'Don't let me keep you from your champagne and vol-au-vents. I'm in the process of finding myself somewhere to live, and I've several properties to view.'

At that precise moment Laurel wasn't remotely interested in where he chose to live. She couldn't have cared less if he took a quick trip to the bottom of the River Ouse, and she fervently wished he would take himself back to Boston, Massachusetts, and let her life, by some miracle, be transported back to where it stood before he came into it.

While she was still busy thinking of something witty and scathing to say, which he couldn't immediately cap with a more clever remark, his features relaxed into that fascinating smile that was beginning to haunt her reveries.

'Have a nice weekend,' he said. 'See you Monday. Don't be late. Castleford only employs workers, not shirkers.'

Laurel watched him go, striding out briskly, his tailored Aquascutum trenchcoat slung casually over one arm. How she hated him!

Or did she? However much she told herself it was no more than smart opportunism, she now remembered the calm sympathy in his eyes as they had sat by the glowing fire. The electric response which snapped and crackled along her nerves whenever he came within touching distance.

If her father had had to sell Caterplus to anyone, why, in the name of all that was sacred, couldn't it have been to someone she could have hated wholeheartedly?

CHAPTER FOUR

LAUREL sat at the desk in her office, toying abstractedly with a pencil. Before her on the desk-top lay two terse notes from Trent Castleford, no more than four lines each in length, but bristling with orders she was required to carry out.

He had been MD at Caterplus for six weeks, and for Laurel they had been the longest and the hardest of her life. She couldn't precisely say why.

It wasn't that he had given her personally a hard time. He demanded hard work, but that she had never stinted on, and, much as she would have found a grim satisfaction in believing he expected more of her than he did of any of her colleagues, she could not point to any real evidence backing up such a contention.

It was true that he had implemented changes, but there had not been the wholesale overturning of every established practice that many had feared. After six weeks, Laurel sensed a collective easing of breath around the corridors, and wondered wretchedly why she could not exhale more freely along with it.

Gloria, whom Trent had inherited as personal secretary from Robert, was still occupying that position, and had given her new boss the tentative thumbs-up.

'Although one has to be mentally on one's toes all the time,' she admitted to Laurel. 'I thought your father was exacting enough, but TFC—wow, he expects everything done perfectly, and preferably yesterday! He knows exactly what he's dictated to me, and if I change so much

as a word he notices. Unless I can convince him that
what I've typed is better than what *he* said—and I usually
can't—I'm in trouble. But he's fair, and straight-
forward. Funny too, on occasion.'

Funny? Laurel had grimaced. 'You mean that man
has a sense of humour?'

'Oh, come on, Laurel, you must have noticed—
everyone else has!' Gloria protested. 'He's dry, and
comes out with the weirdest comments absolutely
straight-faced. Like in the management meeting the other
day, when Alan suggested that if we gave the poultry
suppliers one more stiff warning they might start making
their deliveries on time, TFC said——'

'I know, I was there,' Laurel interrupted, a trifle
wearily. 'He said there was more chance of the *Titanic*
coming up with survivors. Ha, ha! Consequently, we're
to have a new supplier. Golden Farms have supplied
Caterplus since the early days—the chairman is a personal friend of my father. I didn't vote for the change.'

Laurel sighed, recalling the meeting, Trent's cool gaze
dissecting her across the board table, before, with calm
impersonality, he invited a vote that went against her.

'It's getting to be a major problem, Laurel,' Stewart
Ballard, the production manager, had said apologetically. 'I can't plan schedules when I can't rely on deliveries.' And she had seen clearly that all her father's
old team were reluctantly nodding in assent. *Deserting
me, every one*, she had thought bitterly.

'You stuck your neck out there, didn't you?' Alan had
remarked gently, later. 'Was that wise . . . or even necessary, on that issue?'

'On a public relations basis, I believe it was,' Laurel
defended herself stoutly. 'Loyalty and length of associ-
ation have to stand for something.'

The accountant had raised an eyebrow. 'So you weren't just being obstructionist for the sake of it?' he queried softly.

'Why should I do that?' Laurel demanded sharply, and he shook his head.

'I don't know, Laurel. *You* tell me. One thing's for sure—your father has gone, and Castleford is here. You have to accept it.'

'The King is dead—long live the King,' Laurel said drily, but she was not blind to the warning in Alan's quiet words. If she wanted to take on Trenton Foxley-Castleford and win, she had to be on safer ground than she had been over the suppliers. She knew why he had not troubled to demolish her personally. He had been so certain of his support from other managers that he had not needed to lower himself. His dismissive, 'Next item?' had spoken volumes of amused condescension. She wasn't in his league.

With all her heart she wished Robert and Ana were at home. She missed Ana's comforting, uncritical support, and, for all their disagreements, surely Robert would have been prepared to talk problems over with her? But the break had been complete. Two days after retiring and transferring Caterplus to Castleford Industries, Robert had flown to Miami with Ana to begin their Caribbean cruise.

There was only Clive to go home to at night, and he was more of a liability than a help, Laurel thought morosely.

'You used to be a real fun kid,' he had complained when she walked in and flung herself into a chair, her head pounding from the tension of another day's fear that she would put a foot wrong, her nerves screaming for a release she could not find. 'Now you're turning into a grumpy old shrew! What's happened to you?'

'In three words—Trenton Foxley-Castleford,' she retorted angrily. 'It's all very fine for you! All you have to do all day is lie about watching videos, or go to the pub or the races! You don't have to force yourself every day to do a job you used to love, waiting all the time for *that man* to find some fault and pounce on you for it!'

Clive swung his feet off the sofa and sat up, scattering papers and magazines.

'Then why don't you leave, if you hate this bloke so much, and can't cope?' he asked equably. 'It's only a job, after all. There must be others.'

'Must there? If so, *you* don't seem to be having much success finding one,' she had been unable to resist flinging back nastily. 'And who said I couldn't cope?'

Leave? Leave Caterplus? Throw in her hand and give up so easily? No doubt that would give Trent Castleford immense satisfaction.

A deep sigh had escaped Laurel. No, it wouldn't. He would simply shrug and set about finding someone, probably from within his vast organisation, to replace her. She simply wasn't that important in his scheme of things. Was that what irked her? Did she want him to come out gunning for her rather than sit back and wait for her to shoot herself in the foot?

Clive had grinned—almost leered at her, putting Laurel instantly on her guard, with memories of New Year's Eve. She had never felt able to be truly relaxed with him since then.

'I reckon you've got the hots for this man Castleford, and he isn't paying you enough attention,' he said.

Laurel had sat bolt upright.

'Don't be ridiculous!' she had said scathingly, trying to ignore the fact that he had only stated in cruder language something uncannily similar to her own thoughts.

Although she feared Trent's power and influence, and told herself frequently that she hated him, below the surface of her emotions that latent physical attraction still simmered uncomfortably and would not be doused. His cool, questioning stare across a room made her pulse falter. If he leaned over her desk to read a document, she caught the tang of his aftershave mingled with the warmth of his body, and a strange weakness assailed her, so that she had to concentrate hard on what he was saying. Often she found herself watching his strong, capable hands gesturing to outline a point he was making, and briefly she would imagine them touching and stroking her, and she tingled intimately.

He had never again referred to their snowbound Christmas meeting, and she could only assume he had dismissed it from his mind. The information she had unwittingly given him he had stored and used for his own purpose. No doubt if she had been willing he would have taken her to bed to enliven a dull hour or two for him—and then as quickly forgotten that too.

Laurel shook herself. The instructions Trent had left on her desk this afternoon he would expect her to have well in hand by lunchtime tomorrow, and if she had failed to set matters in motion he would want to know why. She could not afford to relax for a second, would not give him the opportunity of coming down on her like a ton of bricks.

And she had to stop harking back to that first meeting. It had meant nothing to him, beyond a fortuitous opportunity to learn more about the company he was planning to take over. For her as a woman he had perhaps felt a passing attraction, but maybe he had only been bored and lonely, lacking the company of some special person at a time when everyone else was with friends, family—or lovers.

Well, she couldn't be that special, if he was prepared to cheat on her casually, Laurel mused darkly. But then they said men could do that—indulge in light, meaningless sex without disturbing their deeper feelings.

She shivered. About deeper feelings, and about the dangerous minefields of sexual relationships, she knew very little. All her own involvements to date had been light and short-lived. A sociable girl who enjoyed friendships with both sexes, none the less Laurel had a serious core, and she had devoted it chiefly to her work. Her love had been given only to her family, and no man had done more than scrape the surface of her feelings so far. It might well be unfashionable to be a virgin at twenty-one, but Laurel had never let this trouble her.

Until now, when she was entertaining these strange longings and crazy fantasies about a man whose arrival on the scene had changed her life for the worse. A man she still could not help resenting, against whom she was still fighting a rearguard resistance she knew in her heart she could not win.

With a disgusted sigh, Laurel picked up the telephone receiver and set about the first of the tasks that same man had given her. There was little to be gained by inviting trouble.

That evening she arrived home to find Clive out, and the house in a state of chaos, despite the fact that Ana's twice-weekly cleaning lady had given it a thorough going-over only the previous day. The kitchen was a disgrace, the sink piled high with dirty mugs and glasses, cupboard doors gaping open, half-empty cans of baked beans and discarded soup packets everywhere. The lounge was awash with crumpled newspapers, beer cans and articles of dirty clothing which had not made it to the linen basket, and there was an unpleasant odour of stale cigarette smoke. Several packs of cards scattered untidily on the floor indicated that a poker session had recently taken place.

Laurel took off her jacket, rolled up her sleeves, and set to work with a will, anger bubbling up fiercely inside her as she worked. The culprit arrived home halfway through her clean-up operation, and she rounded on him immediately.

'Do you think this is fair?' she demanded furiously. 'If you must have card parties, at least you don't have to leave the place looking like a Wild West saloon! And all those dirty mugs! Clive, is it too much trouble to load the dishwasher, for Pete's sake?'

She picked up a pair of discarded socks and, holding them at arm's length, marched through to the utility-room to deposit them in the basket.

'You didn't have to do all that,' he said sheepishly on her return. 'Some of the lads came round, and—well, it developed. I'd have cleaned up eventually.'

'Oh, yes? You mean you'd have left it for Mrs Harvey, who isn't due again until Friday,' Laurel said scornfully. She sighed, her anger running its course swiftly, as ever, and subsiding. 'Clive, it's not the first time,' she continued more quietly. 'I can't be expected to put in a full day's hard slog and come home to *this*. Besides, you really ought to find a job.'

He smiled beguilingly.

'Sorry, kiddo. I am trying, but no one has the right outlet for a man of my multiple talents,' he excused himself blithely.

Laurel couldn't resist a grin. She had seen the evidence of his endeavours when she'd come in. In the labour-starved south-east of England, it was difficult to believe he couldn't find something.

'Perhaps, until the ideal opportunity comes along, you could take on something temporary to keep you going?' she suggested diplomatically. 'Why don't I see if I can find you a job at Caterplus?'

'Hell's bells! Doing what?' he asked suspiciously. '*I* don't want to end up a nervous wreck like you!'

'*You* wouldn't necessarily have to come into contact with Trent Castleford every day,' she pointed out grimly. 'You could drive a delivery van, for instance. That wouldn't be too onerous.'

He brightened. 'I wouldn't mind that. Get out and about,' he said. 'To be honest, I'm getting a bit bored with sitting around here, and the guys damn near bankrupted me today!'

Laurel resolved to get him a job on the delivery vans, but decided to cover herself by mentioning her intention to Trent before doing anything else. She didn't want him accusing her of going behind his back, finding positions with the company for members of her family.

As luck would have it, she had the perfect excuse for seeing him that morning, to report on the progress she had achieved on the tasks he had set her. She phoned Gloria, who gave her a time when Trent could spare her five minutes, and accordingly took herself along to his office at the appointed hour.

Trent's inner sanctum was reached via his secretary's outer office.

'He's just popped out to see Alan,' said Gloria, waving her through. 'Go in and take a seat. He won't be long.'

Robert had always made a practice of leaving the connecting door open, closing it only when he wanted to talk privately to someone, and Trent seemed to be following the same custom. The door was open, so Laurel left it that way, leaving Trent to judge whether what they had to say required privacy or not.

She had been sitting there a minute or two when one of the battery of phones on Trent's desk rang. At first she took no notice, assuming Gloria would come in and answer it, but it rang again, several times, and it dawned on Laurel that Gloria must have left her office.

The phone rang once more, imperatively. It was the direct, private external line which did not go through the switchboard, and whoever was on the other end was not going to give up. Laurel hesitated only fractionally before picking it up, and she did not have time to announce herself to the caller before a curt, impatient voice barked out, 'Trent? Goddammit, I've been trying to reach you all morning!'

Laurel did not recognise the voice, but she thought she would not like to be on the owner's bad books!

'This is Mr Castleford's office,' she said clearly, 'but he's not here at the moment. Can I help you?'

'I should doubt it!' the voice rasped back harshly. 'This is J.J. Castleford, and I want to speak to my son. Like now!'

Laurel, stunned by the abrupt, brusque manner of the head of the organisation for whom she now worked, had just begun to stammer out, 'I'll see if I can——' when a footfall distracted her, and she looked up, relieved, to see Trent coming in, immaculate as ever, today in a navy pinstripe suit and a shirt of brilliant white.

Covering the mouthpiece with her hand, she said quietly, 'It's Mr Castleford senior.'

Trent cast a glance of resigned supplication towards the ceiling, and took the receiver from her hand. When Laurel half rose, intending to leave them to talk privately, he motioned her imperiously back into her seat, obliging her to remain. Perching on the edge of the desk, he said only, 'Pop?'

For a good two minutes, a tirade waxed from the other end of the line, of which Laurel could not hear the gist, only the brusque, angry voice rapping out at some length. Finally there was a pause, and Trent said with heavy sarcasm, 'Good to hear from you too, Pop. How's Boston? How's Mom? Yes, I'm fine.'

This facetious line obviously enraged J.J. Castleford even further, and he ranted on a while longer. Laurel watched the amusement fade from Trent's eyes, and his jaw harden.

'Now just hold on a while, *sir*,' he said, with faint but intentional emphasis on the last word. 'As I told you last week, it's all going absolutely according to plan. There's no problem whatsoever.'

The voice at the other end sounded marginally calmer, and after a while Trent nodded, a grim little smile playing around his mouth. 'Well, Peters would say that, wouldn't he? He's waiting for me to fall flat on my...' pausing, he quirked an eyebrow at Laurel, and finished '...face.'

She looked down at the desk top, her ivory skin flushing pink. She could hardly not have heard what was said, but his glance accused her plainly of betraying her interest a little too overtly.

She avoided Trent's eyes, but did not miss the hard resolve in his voice as he said, 'Either *I'm* handling this end or *he* is. Since I'm the one this side of the pond, he can get off my back. No, you don't need to tell him that, I'll do so myself.'

There was another pause, then Trent said laconically, 'OK, Pop. Cheerio—love to Mom.'

Laurel looked up again at that, in time to see him replace the receiver. Should she be surprised that Trent Castleford loved his mother? Most people did. It certainly sounded as if his relationship with his father was far more abrasive. Meeting the guarded tawny eyes of the golden boy, Laurel had a sudden swift intimation that even for the sons of heads of empires it was not always that easy.

'It was unfortunate for you that you had to get my father on one of his less pleasant days,' he said smoothly. 'Gloria shouldn't have left the office unattended. I won't have that.'

Laurel saw that Gloria was in for a rocket, at the very least.

'There are times when all of us have to leave the office,' she said placatingly. 'And it wasn't unattended—I was here.'

Momentarily, a smile transformed him back to the Renaissance prince, and Laurel felt something odd happen to her solar plexus.

'You do a strong line of loyalty, don't you, Laurel?' he said quietly. 'Just remember, on your progress up the career ladder, not to give it unreservedly or expect it always to be appreciated or returned.'

She knew he was referring to the telephone call he had just taken, and disbelievingly she said, 'You mean...your father?'

Trent shook his head.

'No. Pop is hard, and we don't always agree, but he's straight. But there are those on the board at Castleford

Industries who'd have my hide on a plate if they could, and they like to whisper in his ear.'

Laurel frowned.

'But surely... you're his son. They can't harm you.'

Trent slid from his perch, closed the communicating door, and turned to face her, hands in the pockets of his suit jacket. His face was unrevealing, a mask of invulnerability which his words belied.

'If you believe that, you're more naïve than I thought,' he said crisply. 'Castleford Industries is a vast organisation with shareholders to answer to. Sure, my father is founder and chairman, but seats on the board aren't given away. They have to be fought for.' Anticipating her response, he nodded. 'Yes, even mine. Especially mine. I've something to prove, just as you have.'

For a moment they looked at one another soberly, and in that brief, wordless exchange of thoughts Laurel reached, if not a turning point, then at least a signpost towards one. She had not, she knew, entirely done fighting Trent Castleford. But perhaps she acknowledged that, even for him, the skies of business were not clear blue, the paths not all strewn with roses. There were those who resented his success, his progress, those whom *he* had to overcome in order to be where he was. A glimmer of kinship awoke in her a guarded sympathy and she edged her way, very cautiously, towards a *modus vivendi* in which they could work together.

Quite suddenly Trent broke the tenuous contact between them, sliding into the chair behind his desk and becoming once again, and irrevocably, her boss.

'Right. Fill me in on the progress with this Southern Inns contract,' he ordered briskly.

The call from J.J. Castleford and her brief insight into Trent's problems had all but driven from Laurel's mind the business of finding a job for Clive. Only as they finished discussing the matter under consideration did she recall her earlier intention, and, about to leave, she turned back to look at Trent.

'There was something else——'

'Um? What's that?' He was already studying a sheaf of typewritten reports, and might almost have forgotten her existence, let alone her presence in his office.

'There's this...relative of mine.' She didn't want to go into the details of her relationship to Clive. 'He's looking for a temporary job while he...sorts out his career prospects.'

She stifled a grimace. Oh, boy, Laurel, that's the biggest PR con of the decade, she thought.

'So?' Trent sounded impatient, and she pressed on swiftly.

'Well, I thought perhaps he could drive one of our delivery vans. We're generally short of drivers.'

'Good grief, Laurel!' His irritation was plainly visible. 'You hardly needed to ask me about that! Get your relative to call and see Ken Newall in Despatch. The vans are his baby—as you should well know.'

He bent his head over the reports once more, without another word, and it was obvious to Laurel that she was dismissed. Obvious, also, that once again she had gone about things the wrong way—although this time with the best of intentions. Would she ever learn to read him? Or would whatever she said or did be wrong in his eyes? Maybe she had only imagined, for a moment, that he understood and sympathised with how she felt, having to prove her worth all the time.

There's no way we can understand one another, she thought bleakly, and it depressed her beyond words.

Her depression changed swiftly to anger the next day, when Clive, having jauntily breezed into Despatch asking for a job driving the vans, was promptly turned down. He knew his way around Caterplus well enough to find Laurel's office, and, bursting in on her, he voiced his grievance in no uncertain terms.

'The blighter refused to set me on!' he declared furiously. 'Said it was because I had too many points against me on my driving licence! I told him they were only for speeding, and it's easy to speed in an MG, but he wouldn't have it. New rule, he said—TFC insists on clean licences—but squeaky clean!'

Laurel rested her head in her hands and groaned. 'I'm sorry, Clive—I didn't know about that or I wouldn't have suggested it,' she said. 'Wasn't there anything else they could offer you?'

Clive snorted.

'Oh, yes! Packing—putting things in boxes! I told him where to stick that! I'm not so desperate!' He glared at her. 'Well, thanks a bunch, kid!' he said angrily. 'In future, don't do me any favours!'

He was shouting so loudly his voice had to be audible clear down the corridor. Laurel was not surprised when her office door opened, but her self-esteem plummeted still further when she saw whose attention had been attracted by the commotion.

'Young man,' Trent Castleford said icily, 'two things. One—I won't tolerate this kind of rowdy behaviour within a mile of any establishment I run. Two—I don't take kindly to having members of my staff harassed. Now get your butt out of here!'

He never raised his voice, and his gaze remained arctic-cool, but Laurel saw Clive's bravado deflate to ineffectuality before her eyes. He looked at Trent, his jaw

dropped open, and Laurel knew that he had recognised
the other man from New Year's Eve at the Golf Club.
Accusingly, his glance swung back to Laurel, before he
flung out of the office, and stomped off down the
corridor.

Trent did not move, but his eyebrows rose questioningly, and Laurel knew he was waiting for an
explanation.

'He...he came for a job on the vans,' she said lamely.
'Remember...I asked you about it yesterday? Ken Newall
turned him down because of a speeding infringement.'

There was a sudden knowing glitter in the hard eyes
regarding her.

'Ken acted quite correctly,' he said. 'Wasn't that the
young man I saw you with at the Golf Club? For relative, read "boyfriend". The subterfuge was hardly
necessary, Laurel. I don't expect my female employees
to be apprentice nuns.'

Beneath the cool ivory skin the pink flush glowed
bright, and there was nothing she could do to hide it.

'I wasn't...he isn't...' she began, disgusted at the
mental disarray into which he had thrown her. Her
mouth clamped shut. If she explained her precise
relationship to Clive now, it would become obvious that
she had deliberately misled him about the same subject
on New Year's Eve. And why would she do that, unless
it were to arouse his interest, jealousy, attraction? Laurel
was in a cleft stick, and she had the uncomfortable sensation that he was enjoying watching her wriggle.

'Laurel, I'm not remotely interested in your...er...
romantic life,' he said, with contemptuous amusement.
'So long as you confine it to out-of-office hours, that's
fine by me. OK?'

He closed the door quietly behind him, leaving her sitting fuming at her desk, face burning, hands clenched tightly, nails digging into her palms.

She hated him! Right now she detested Trent Castleford fiercely and wholeheartedly, without reservations. Hated Clive too, for dropping her into such an embarrassing muddle. And Ken Newall for sticking religiously to his newly imposed rules.

'Damn all men,' she muttered crossly to herself.

Later on, when she had cooled off, she told herself that Clive was just Clive—boyish, irresponsible, occasionally funny and often exasperating. The exasperation factor was increasing in ratio to the amusing, lately, but basically he hadn't changed, and wasn't likely to. She could not stay indefinitely angry with him, the mental effort required was too great, and he simply wasn't worth it.

Nor could she really blame poor Ken for obeying management orders expressly given, especially when he rang her up and told her he was sorry, but he'd had no option.

'I've known young Clive since he was a boy,' he said regretfully. 'Bit of a tearaway, but there's no real harm in him. But rules are rules, and you'll appreciate I couldn't make an exception, even to please you.'

'That's all right, Ken,' sighed Laurel. 'It's my fault—I should have checked it out before sending him along to see you. There are a number of new rules lately.'

'Most of them reasonable, Miss Laurel, if you don't mind my saying so,' Ken pointed out. 'Those vans go all over the county, and what they carry is our livelihood. And our reputation. TFC is only looking out for Caterplus in his own way, just as Mr Robert did in his. If you see what I mean.'

Laurel saw. Another convert to the gospel according to Trent Castleford, she thought, as she put down the phone. Very soon her worst fears were going to prove unfounded, and Caterplus would be a united and happy company, working cheerfully and efficiently under its new helmsman.

Well and good, for everyone but her. For it would appear that she was the only member of staff giving the impression of being discontented and uncooperative. And that was ironic, for only yesterday she had seen a glimmer of light, and promised herself that she would do her best to work with Trent, not in spite of him.

Now, after that episode with Clive in her office, he thought she was an immature, misguided ninny who couldn't even keep her affairs separate from her work! And it seemed she had a long, long way to go to persuade him to take her seriously.

She told herself it was only for career reasons that his good opinion mattered so desperately, that she hated him and did not otherwise give a fig what he thought of her personally. Over and over again she told herself, as if constant repetition could make it so: I hate Trent Castleford, I don't care what he thinks of me, and I am certainly *not* attracted to him.

Why, then, didn't she believe it?

CHAPTER FIVE

CLIVE had plenty to say about his encounter with Trent in Laurel's office, most of it uncomplimentary.

'My uncle built that company from scratch, and I object to being talked down to by some loud-mouthed Yank!' he declared truculently.

These were sentiments Laurel had admitted to herself, but oddly enough, she now found herself defending Trent's position.

'He's not American—well, only half,' she said wearily. 'His father, J.J. Castleford, is as English as you or I. As for being loud-mouthed, you were the one doing all the shouting.'

'I see,' Clive said meaningfully. 'Changed sides, have we? Come down from the high moral ground? It's easy to see why. You forbore to tell me Castleford was the man you were giving the glad eye at the Golf Club! It was obvious then that it was only a matter of time before you succumbed to his charms.'

'I haven't succumbed to anything,' Laurel protested heatedly. 'It's purely a business relationship—there's nothing else going on.'

Clive bit into his prawn cracker—Laurel, feeling unable even to consider cooking that night, had brought home a Chinese takeaway—and gave a suggestive wink.

'But you'd like there to be, wouldn't you?' he persisted. 'Don't try to fool me, Laurel. I've known you too long, and I recognise that look in a woman's eyes.

He turns you on. What I'd really like to know is—just what has he got that I haven't?'

Laurel prodded uneasily at her sliced beef and water chestnuts, trying to suppress the reply that sprang instantly to her mind.

Trent Castleford, for all his faults, his arrogance and his sense of his own superiority, was a man, whereas Clive was in reality no more than an overgrown schoolboy. Women were attracted to men who *did* things, made things move. However, she wasn't about to admit that there was an ounce of truth in Clive's accusation that she had what he so crudely called 'the hots' for the new managing director.

'Trent is my boss, Clive, that's all he is, and I'm stuck with him, whether I like it or not,' she said soberly. 'You're the boy I grew up with. We used to be friends, and I'd like to keep it that way.'

'That's the trouble, Laurel, in a nutshell—we've grown up,' he said. 'I'd like for us to play more grown-up games.'

'The only game I'm going to play with you is Trivial Pursuit, or maybe Scrabble,' she said firmly. She pushed aside the foil containers. 'You can finish the chicken fried rice—I'm not hungry.'

That night she slipped the bolt on her bedroom door. Doing so made her feel mean-spirited. Surely Clive wouldn't . . . well, force himself on her? Would he? But they were alone in the house, and she wasn't taking any chances. How she wished Robert and Ana were here, but all she had of them were postcards showing white beaches with waving palm trees and turquoise seas.

It was ironic. She was alone every night with her childhood friend who had suddenly decided to take an unwelcome interest in her as a woman. Her days were spent under the same roof as a man for whom she felt an increasing if fiercely resisted attraction, who seemed entirely unaware of her in that sense, despite what had taken place at their first meeting.

'I've a titbit of information you might find interesting,' Gloria said to her, a few days later. 'Our new lord and master was once a married man.'

Laurel glanced up quickly—they were in her office—guiltily checking that the door was closed.

'Should you be gossiping about your boss's private life at all?' she queried.

'Really, Laurel, it's hardly classified info,' Gloria protested. 'He must be in his thirties. Most men have tested the water by then.'

'And he told you he'd been married?' Laurel could not resist asking.

'Lord, no—he never talks about that sort of thing. But this woman rang up asking for him, when he was out. I asked her name so he could phone her back, and she said she was Cara Peretta—aka the former Mrs Trent Castleford.'

Gloria paused triumphantly, but Laurel merely shrugged.

'So? The great TFC has an ex.' She assumed supreme indifference. 'One can well understand why she couldn't hack being married to him, and got herself out!'

'Come on, Laurel, don't you know who Cara Peretta is?' Gloria persisted, with a superior grin. 'And you living just down the road from Glyndebourne, so to speak! She's an opera singer—a very famous one.'

'I don't follow opera.' Laurel digested this piece of news thoughtfully. Trent Castleford married to a singer, an artiste? What a potentially explosive combination, she thought. It was hardly surprising it hadn't worked,

if her ego was as powerful as his! She found the notion
intriguing, and throughout the day it kept returning to
haunt her.

Cara Peretta. The name sounded romantic—Italian,
perhaps? Was she very beautiful, as well as gifted? Laurel
wondered. Had Trent loved her very much? She remembered the faint aura of loneliness she had picked up on
their first meeting. Could it be that he was still a little
in love with his ex-wife?

You're letting your imagination run away with you,
she told herself sternly. All this had nothing to do with
her. Whatever Trent felt or did not feel for the mysterious Cara, of whose existence she had known nothing
until that morning, it was none of her concern.

Nevertheless, she found herself looking at him with
new eyes. Here was a man who must once have loved a
woman deeply, and, since he had gone through the
rigours of a divorce, presumably a man who had also
suffered. It was a novel thought.

'Do I have a smut on my nose or something, Laurel?'
he asked her with gentle amusement. 'If so, I do wish
you'd tell me instead of looking at me as if I'd suddenly
sprouted pink hair from my ears!'

She started. Had it been so obvious that she was
studying him?

'Sorry—I was thinking of something else,' she muttered apologetically.

No, it wasn't pink hair or smuts on noses she had discovered, but something more subtle, but much more disturbing. Feelings. Emotions. A life that had not just
sprung into being when Trent had walked into the
Caterplus building, but which was already full, vibrant
and three-dimensional. He had a mother he was very
fond of, a father he respected but with whom he did not

always see eye to eye...corporate enemies who were after his blood...and he had once been married to an operatic diva. Trent Castleford was rounding out before her eyes, and she wasn't sure she could handle the full power of his persona. Shivery sensations when he came close to her were one thing—interest in him as a real human being was quite another.

At five twenty-five that afternoon, Laurel was just tidying her desk preparatory to going home. Over the past few days she had invented as many excuses as possible to get herself out of the house in the evening. She had visited friends, talked others into visits to the cinema, gone to an art exhibition in Brighton where the paintings reminded her of the offerings children brought home from playschool. Tonight she had no plans, and had run out of excuses. She had to spend the evening at home, and could only hope that Clive would take himself to one of his clubs or favourite pubs where his friends congregated.

But he'd done little of that lately. 'Shortage of funds,' he'd replied briefly when she had asked him why he spent so much time at home, but Laurel was puzzled. True, he had no wages coming in at the moment, but his parents had left him well provided for. It was unlike him to curtail his social activities.

It was difficult and far from enjoyable to have to sit watching TV or pretending to read a book, with the uneasy feeling that one of these nights he was going to make a pass at her, and she was going to have to slap him down, with all the attendant unpleasantness that would involve. Since New Year's Eve it had been rather like waiting for the other shoe to drop. Sometimes she wished they could get it over with, and clear the air.

The phone on her desk rang just as she was picking up her jacket, and it was Trent.

'Laurel, I've got a job for you,' he said tersely.

'Now?' she queried, surprised, and he replied a little sharply,

'Yes—now, unless you're one of those types I don't usually employ, who watch the minute hand on the clock.'

'Certainly not,' she said in a crisp denial.

'Come along to my office and I'll explain it to you in person,' he ordered, and rang off.

Laurel fought a sudden bout of extreme nervousness. What was it he wanted her to do? Could she cope with it? No one else had ever afflicted her with these attacks of self-doubt in an area where she had always had confidence, inspiring her at the same time with a fierce need to prove her abilities.

Five minutes ago she had been reluctant to go home. Now home seemed like a welcome refuge, and she wanted to cut and run. Nothing Clive could do induced in her the mixture of anxiety and taut expectation that every encounter with Trent brought about. She could cope with Clive. With Trent, she could barely hold her own.

She found him seated at his desk, in shirt-sleeves.

'You can go now, Gloria,' he said to his secretary, as she placed a tray with coffee, cream, sugar and two cups on the desk in front of him.

'You're sure?'

'Sure. Run along, I shan't need you any more,' he assured her. 'Take a seat, Laurel—and you can be mother, as they say.'

Alone with him in the office, Laurel poured coffee, noting that he took his black and sugarless. She wondered apprehensively what all this was about, and he did not leave her very long in suspense.

'JJ just rang up from Boston,' he said, with a wry grin. 'My father makes no allowances for time differences, or such ephemera. What he wants is a profile of, say, half a dozen Caterplus outlets—description, turnover, nature of operation—chapter and verse. He wants the information to catch, and I quote, "the next available mail".'

Laurel glanced at the clock.

'It's just as well that tonight's has gone!' she said with a short laugh. 'It will have to be tomorrow morning.'

The sudden appreciative smile he cast her lifted her spirits quite disproportionately.

'Attagirl, as they used to say in all the best kids' comics,' he said. 'I figured you'd be the best person to dig out the details. Vary it, Laurel. What we're trying to build is a composite picture of the Caterplus operation. When you've sorted it out, bring it back to me and we'll knock it into final shape.'

She went swiftly back to her own office on a wave of confidence. *This* she could do, probably better than anyone in the company. She visited the outlets regularly, knew them so well that she only needed to tap them out on her computer to confirm details she already knew. With these to hand, she set about writing a description of the six different customers she had chosen—a traditional country inn, a busy town centre pub, a medium-sized office cafeteria, a gourmet-inclined directors' dining-room, a family-orientated steak house which was a member of a chain, and a roadside café frequented by long-distance drivers.

Her reports were detailed and comprehensive, and she completely forgot the passage of time. It was after seven when she finally took the finished work back to Trent's office. The corridors were hushed and silent, the rooms she passed were all empty. Only under Trent's door a light gleamed, and she was sure he and she were quite alone in the building.

So what? she asked herself, controlling the tremor of her hand as she rapped lightly on his door. Trent wasn't likely to take advantage of that solitude to try and make love to her. They had been working together for more than two months, and in all that time he had not betrayed the slightest interest in her.

But if he did? If he were to kiss her as he had done in the hall of the snowbound inn, if he were to touch her as he had then . . . with the difference, now, that they were alone and unlikely to be interrupted? What would she do? She didn't think he would be an easy man to slap down . . . even if she wanted to do so, and she was far from sure of that!

Laurel braced herself and went in. Trent's desk was awash with papers, he had loosened his tie, and his hair, for once, was rumpled, giving him a vulnerable air that was oddly appealing, for all she knew it was illusory.

'I hope I didn't take too long,' she said diffidently, her doubts suddenly returning.

'I'd rather have the job done right,' he said. 'We have plenty of time. The mail doesn't go until tomorrow morning.'

She shivered, he noted it, and, looking at her with a strange, penetrating intentness, he smiled slowly and said, 'Was that because the central heating went off at five-thirty, or at the prospect of being here all night?'

His smile came the closest yet to the one she recalled from their first meeting, and Laurel felt as if someone were inching a hand up her back, slowly, vertebra by vertebra, so that every interstice tingled. She sat down—he hadn't invited her to, but she felt that she must, because her spine was too weak to support her.

'Don't worry, we won't be here all night,' he said, and she had an uncomfortable feeling that he was laughing at her, at her youth, her inexperience, her palpable nervousness. With an enormous effort she straightened in her seat, tightened her lips, and pushed the reports towards him.

Immediately the laughter was gone, and he was all professionalism, grilling Laurel thoroughly on every aspect of what she had written, asking questions she had not thought to answer, refining and reshaping until he was satisfied with the end product. If she had ever wondered what abilities had put him where he was, she no longer did. The thorough, incisive mind stretched her every inch of the way, leaving her uncomfortably aware that he now knew almost as much about her job as she did herself.

'I'll run off the final version on Gloria's word-processor,' she said quietly. Flexibility, Trent had once said he demanded of his staff. Oddly, it did not occur to her now to resent the fact that he had sent Gloria home. Since Laurel herself could formulate and type up the reports, there would have been little point in her staying behind too.

'I think you'd better use yours. I'll need this one,' he said, and she could not hide her surprise.

'You? But...'

'You didn't imagine your reports were all JJ demanded?' he asked wryly, indicating the pile of papers on his desk.

Laurel frowned sympathetically. 'I get the impression he doesn't spare anyone who works for him,' she remarked.

'He certainly does not. Least of all me,' Trent replied practically, and without a trace of self-pity or recrimination in his voice. 'That's how Castleford Industries was born, and how JJ made his millions.'

And, no matter how many times she replayed that speech in her mind, Laurel was never sure whether she heard, or only imagined, that very, very faint note of sarcasm in the last words.

It was well after eight by the time they finished, and she secured the papers in a large, firm envelope addressed to J.J. Castleford at his home address in Boston, and marked 'private and confidential'.

'There's no way these are going to fall into anyone else's hands,' Trent said grimly. 'They're ammunition for a special meeting of the board.'

Laurel gasped.

'Trent!' she exclaimed involuntarily. 'Those reports I did are going before Castleford's board? They—they have my name on them!'

'Sure they have.' He smiled enigmatically. 'That's fame, baby. *You* did the work, you get the credit. That is, if what we did tonight convinces the board that Caterplus is a viable organisation, worthy of greater funding, and I'm the right man to spearhead the European operation. On the other hand, should they fail to do so, you'll go down with me.'

The smile, and his voice, were teasing, but she sensed the seriousness beneath the levity as he said, 'Want to unseal the envelope?'

She took a deep breath.

'No. I stand by what I wrote, and I guess you know what you're doing. Only—I had no idea it was that important.'

Trent switched off all the lights behind them as they left the building. Outside, the early March night was crisp and cold, but there was a scent in the air that heralded the approach of spring, not too far around the corner. The security man wished them goodnight as they walked across the car park.

'I do hope,' said Trent, politely poker-faced, 'that you had nothing arranged for this evening.'

'Would it have mattered if I had?' Laurel laughed. 'I notice you didn't ask me before.'

'I'm not that gentlemanly. I'd have had to insist you cancel.' He looked down at her from his height, his eyes gleaming, reflecting the frosty moonlight. 'You don't think I've a gentlemanly bone in my body, do you?'

'Once I thought you had,' she heard herself say, disbelieving her own provocative audacity.

'Then I'll prove first impressions were right,' he said. 'I've kept you late—now I'll feed you.'

'Oh, no——' Her protest was automatic, and he ignored it. Taking her arm, he led her out of the car park.

'We'll come back for our respective vehicles later. The place I have in mind is only a short walk,' he said.

They walked up one of the steep, cobbled 'twittens', little lanes which led up the hill towards the high street, flanked by mediaeval houses. Laurel kept pace with his long stride as best she could. She was feeling elated, on a high. Tonight he had needed her, trusted her, and she had succeeded in proving her worth.

Sink or swim, what they had done tonight made co-conspirators of them. She was bound to him, fighting for Caterplus, on his side, against the faceless men in

Boston who opposed him and were out for his blood. And now here she was, going out to dinner with him. Days ago, she would not have believed any of this possible.

Halfway up the hill, Trent stopped at the door of a small restaurant, whose lights glowed warmly secretive from behind maroon velvet curtains.

'This must be a new place,' said Laurel. 'I'm sure I haven't noticed it before.'

'It is. The opening night was only last week,' he told her. 'It's very good—that is, if you like Italian food.'

Something nudged at Laurel's consciousness, and it was strange how her elation ebbed away.

'Love it,' she said mechanically, suddenly thinking of Cara Peretta.

Inside the restaurant, the décor was plain black and white enlivened by tall green palms in tubs, the floor was Travertine marble, and the warmth was pleasant and unobtrusive.

'I hate those imitation trats with checked curtains and candles in Chianti bottles, and posters of Mount Vesuvius,' Trent said cheerfully.

The waiter approached them, and his eyes lit with recognition at the sight of Laurel's companion. He launched into Italian, to which Trent responded briefly but competently, without hesitation, as if the language came to him naturally, like a coat he had not worn for some time, but which still fitted him.

Taking her seat at the table to which they were ushered, Laurel could not resist commenting on this.

'You obviously speak Italian quite fluently,' she said. 'Would it be inquisitive to ask where you learned it? Your family aren't Italian, are they?'

He regarded her steadily over the top of the menu.

'No. My father, as you probably know, hailed originally from Liverpool. My mother's family are Boston Brahmins.' At her puzzled frown, he translated, 'Local nobs, the closest equivalent to aristocracy! As you can imagine, they were none too pleased when their daughter decided to marry this impecunious immigrant, fresh off the boat!'

'But they're happily married, your parents?' Laurel asked.

'Blissfully. A good thing JJ didn't marry for money, for not one cent did he get from Mother's people until he was way past the point where he needed it! I was born in the US, but we moved back over here for a while when I was young, and my education, like my parentage, is mixed—Winchester and Harvard. I think my maternal grandfather fixed the first for me. His old school, don't you know?'

He spoke lightly, half mockingly adopting the tones of the educated English upper classes, and then fell back into the cool mid-Atlantic he used with equal facility.

'But you didn't really want to know all that, did you? You asked about the Italian. I learned that when I studied in Italy. Shall we order?'

After he had given her a fairly full résumé of his family background, it seemed he had no intention of revealing any more intimate connections. She was not to be told anything about Cara Peretta, or his marriage, although obviously this must be where she fitted into the story of his life. Instead, he concentrated firmly on the menu.

'I'm going to have the *caponata* to begin,' he said. 'How about you?'

Laurel knew when she was being deliberately sidetracked. Furthermore, she thought, a trifle sadly, there was nothing celebratory or social about this meal together, and she was foolish ever to have thought that there might be. Trent had kept her working late, and felt obliged to buy her dinner. That was all there was to it. She was here with him, he was being pleasant and companionable, and tonight they had worked together as never before. She ought to be well pleased with the evening's developments, but somehow, for her, the pleasure had already gone from the occasion.

The food was excellent, though. Trent was an expert judge of Italian cooking. From the cold vegetable antipasto of aubergines, celery, tomatoes, olives and pine nuts, to the *timballo di riso con scampi e funghi*—a rice mould, the centre of which was filled with seafood and mushrooms in a delicious sauce—and finally a stunning *cassata alla Siciliana*, a rich gâteau which Laurel complained must be wildly calorific.

'You can take it,' he said, glancing obliquely across the table at her in a manner that made her heart skip stupidly beneath the thin silk of her blouse, and she hoped he did not think she had been blatantly fishing for compliments.

They finished off the half-bottle of dry white Soave and had two cups of very good coffee before Trent signalled to the waiter and in his swift, easy Italian asked for the bill.

'I'm intrigued, I have to confess. What exactly were you studying in Italy?' she asked, daringly risking another cut-off.

'Music,' he said shortly, taking out his credit card and signing the chit, which made Laurel doubly sure she was no more than a legitimate business expense. All kinds of questions chased themselves around in her mind. The pieces of the puzzle were all there, waiting to be assembled. Italy, music, marriage to a singer with an Italian name. But she lacked the fine details of how a hard business supremo like Trent Castleford had happened to be involved in anything so uncharacteristically romantic, and obviously he was not going to tell her. The curtness of his reply indicated quite clearly that all discussion of the subject stopped right there.

They walked in silence back down the hill to the Caterplus car park, and he waited for her to start her car before getting into his own. A touching gesture, she thought—how many men nowadays would bother?—but not strictly necessary.

Seconds later she was eating her words as her engine spluttered and died.

'Damn!' she muttered under her breath, aware of Trent watching her futile efforts to start it with some amusement.

'Laurel,' he said laughingly, 'I think you've been fighting a losing battle with that vehicle for some time. I take it it's a company car?'

'Well, yes.' Robert had offered to buy her a car of her own for her twenty-first birthday, as he'd done for Clive, but she had reasoned that it was pointless, since she did so much work-connected driving and qualified for a company car. Now she was beginning to wish she had accepted the offer.

'Hm. Well, leave it here. We can do something about it in the morning. I'll run you home.'

'I can walk,' she assured him quickly. 'It isn't that far.'

'That would be silly, since my car's here.' He spoke patiently, but with every expectation of being obeyed, and Laurel found herself swiftly installed in the front passenger seat of the quietly luxurious BMW. Trent started the engine—no problems there, it purred to instant life—and automatically slipped a tape in to the deck as they glided out into the street.

A flood of music filled the night, elegant, baroque, and sadly poignant, a woman's fine, soaring contralto voice, effortlessly melodious.

'The late, great Kathleen Ferrier—arguably the best contralto of the century,' Trent said with quiet admiration. 'It's Orpheus' lament from Gluck's *Orfeo*.'

'I've never heard it before, but it's very beautiful,' Laurel said. 'I have to admit that the only kind of opera I'm into is Gilbert and Sullivan.'

He glanced appreciatively sidelong.

'Ignorance isn't a crime, but it takes guts to own up to it,' he said with a smile. 'Actually, I rather enjoy Gilbert and Sullivan, too. I was Nanki-Pooh once, in an amateur production of *The Mikado*, back in Boston.'

Laurel could not suppress a chuckle.

'Sorry—it's just the thought of your mincing about in Japanese costume!' she grinned, and was relieved to see he was laughing too.

'I'll have you know I looked very fetching!' he assured her.

He drove with careful expertise around the one-way system which guided the traffic out of the old town, and followed Laurel's directions. And then, as if he could not prevent himself, as if the music simply took him over, he began to sing along with the tape.

'Eurydice . . . Eurydice . . .

'Oh, hear me . . . oh, answer——'

Laurel's startled gaze shot sideways. He had a magnificent tenor voice, controlled and powerful and quite obviously trained. A voice that could fill a concert hall, unamplified, if released to its full capacity, that knew when to breathe and pause, that used light and shade of sound to brilliant effect. She sat silent, stunned, until the aria ended.

'You have a marvellous voice,' she told him with genuine admiration. 'In fact, I'd say you really ought to be singing professionally.'

A faint, self-deprecating smile tugged the corners of his mouth.

'I thought so too, once,' he said. 'Which way now, Laurel?'

'Oh...' She had been so astounded by his unexpected talent that she had forgotten he did not know where she lived. 'Left...then right. That's it.'

He pulled up outside the house, and for a moment they both sat, saying nothing. She could not divine his thoughts, but had a strong suspicion that they were far away.

'I don't understand,' she said, 'with a gift like that, why you aren't using it?'

Again the strange smile, self-mocking and nostalgic.

'In the world of music, as with most creative endeavour, there's good—and there's great,' he told her. 'I was good. Good enough to know that I'd never be great. It seemed sensible to do something I could excel at, or at least, if I didn't, it wouldn't break my heart. So now I only sing in the car and in the bath.'

Still Laurel did not move to get out of the car. A strange spell kept her transfixed, unable to tear herself away. She wanted—very fiercely—to learn more about this astonishing, many-faceted man, to probe beneath the smooth, hard, cultured surface in search of the deeper springs of his being. To know what really moved him, made him sad, happy, angry, aroused.

But as ever, all he gave her were snippets of himself, and even those he seemed to regret as soon as he had done so.

'We can't sit here all night,' he said firmly. 'Excuse me——' And he reached across her to open the door at her side.

Laurel was rooted to the spot. His face was so close to hers she could feel the warmth of his breath, and his hand accidentally brushed her knee as he reached for the door handle. Then she was looking directly into his eyes, and she felt herself begin to tremble with longing and pent-up anticipation.

'Goodnight, Laurel,' he said quietly, and his lips lightly brushed hers.

He probably meant to do no more than that, she told herself afterwards, a goodnight kiss of the most per- functory kind, which friends and acquaintances ex- changed casually and meaninglessly, these days.

But the instant his mouth touched hers, the dormant, waiting passion in her was released. Her own lips parted involuntarily, and then somehow the kiss became some- thing else. His mouth took hers, which clung and gave willingly, her arms snaked around his neck and his hands closed on her waist, searching their way upwards be- neath her jacket. Her whole body strained against him, fulfilling a need it seemed to have been long denied, arching itself to the touch she had long desired. When he let her go, she was still shivering with the aftermath of that desire.

He was regarding her quizzically, unsmiling, but, she thought, fully aware of the maelstrom he had released in her, and a sudden flood of shame and anger overcame her. How could she have allowed that to happen, how could she have betrayed how deeply he affected her? Behind that calm mask she was sure he was laughing at her, and his cunningly logical mind was probably working out how he could manipulate her helpless attraction to make best use of it.

Without a word, she pushed open the door of the car, stumbled out and slammed it behind her. She did not look back as she ran up the drive, but she heard the engine hum smoothly as he started it up and drove away. Still singing, I'll bet, she thought wretchedly as she fumbled with her key in the lock. Singing and laughing at me! What a fool I am! And one thing's for sure— I'm going to feel even more of a fool when I have to face him in the morning!

CHAPTER SIX

LAUREL perhaps need not have worried. The first person she saw next morning when she arrived at the office was Gloria, who informed her that TFC had gone to London and would be away for a few days.

'But he left this for you,' she said, depositing a small envelope on Laurel's desk, her expression indicating that she already knew what it contained. 'Go on—open it.'

Laurel carefully slit the envelope to reveal a set of car keys, new and shiny.

'The vehicle they belong to is in the car park behind my banger,' Gloria said ruefully, and Laurel looked out of the window, identifying a flame-red saloon as gleaming and pristine as the keys. 'That's your new company car, Laurel. Congratulations. You must have worked especially hard last night,' she added playfully, with a wink.

Laurel aimed a paper-clip at her.

'Don't go spreading that kind of gossip—people are stupid enough to believe it,' she warned. 'There's a simple explanation. My car was playing up yesterday, when I wanted to go home. It wouldn't start—again. But how on earth did he manage to get hold of a new one so quickly?'

'Friends in the trade. He must have been phoning them last night,' said Gloria. 'You're on your way, kid. Castleford Industries is your oyster. And what I said before was meant to be a *joke*. If anyone has earned their place here, you have.'

Laurel smiled, but deep down she thought, I wouldn't be so sure. Trent had appreciated the work she had done on the reports, but had she blown all her efforts by her too eager response to his kiss? He might not want the embarrassment of working with a woman who made it so obvious she found him desirable.

Her contract safeguarded her employment for the rest of the year, but wouldn't prevent him from shunting her off into one of Castleford's other companies. Laurel paled at the thought. When he came back, she must go out of her way to make it clear that kiss had been an isolated impulse, and that she really had no lasting interest in him at all.

'My word!' Clive jeered enviously when she arrived home and parked the red car in the drive. 'What did you have to do to get *that*, one wonders?'

Unlike Gloria, he wasn't joking. Laurel merely sniffed disdainfully and stalked past him indoors.

'You've developed a particularly nasty mind lately,' she said tartly.

'*Moi?*' He feigned surprise. 'Not at all. I'm simply following the evidence of my own eyes. I saw that passionate clinch out there last night. Next thing you'll be giving me that tired old line about working late!'

'Which happens to be the truth. I *had* been working late. Not that it's anything to do with you,' Laurel retorted acidly. 'I didn't know you'd turned into a lace-curtain-twitcher.'

She went straight up to her room without giving him a chance to reply. The situation was becoming intolerable, and she just hoped she could hold on until Robert and Ana arrived home. According to their last postcard, they were on Dominica, and in no hurry to exchange the warmth of the Caribbean for the damp chill of the English winter.

Trent was away from the office until the following Monday, but he sent for Laurel almost immediately he arrived that morning. She straightened her skirt, ran a hand through her shining dark bob of hair, and tried to quieten the painful thudding of her heart.

What did he want? What was he going to say to her? Making her way along the corridor, she played out in her mind a truly awful fantasy in which he told her that he was sorry but she just didn't appeal to him that way, and if she couldn't control her emotions...etcetera, etcetera...

Then she remembered the intensity of his kiss, the urgent way his hands had explored her, and she consoled herself that he couldn't have found her exactly repellent. She hadn't flung herself on him, it had just...happened. Bear up, she told herself as Gloria waved her through, taking heart from the fact that he did not ask her to close the connecting door.

Every time she saw him, it seemed to Laurel that she must have forgotten just how devastatingly attractive he was, because every time he seemed more so, and tiny shock-waves exploded within her. This can't be happening to me, she thought disbelievingly, subsiding on to the chair he indicated, trying hard not to watch the intriguing hollows either side of his jaw, the sudden gleam of the golden irises, the strong, lean hands resting calmly on the desk, fingers intertwined. Remember you are *not* interested, she catechised herself firmly.

But his smile was the open if formal smile of one colleague to another, and if he had given that kiss a second thought there was nothing in his face to say he recalled it now.

'I just wanted to let you know that everything went our way at the board meeting in Boston,' he said crisply. 'For the moment, the opposition has been silenced, although I expect them to go away and start sharpening their knives. Thank you for your help. JJ said he thought your reports were clear and excellently presented.'

Laurel could not conceal her flush of pleasure.

'At least some of the credit for that is yours,' she said.

'I only fine-tuned. The spadework was yours,' he insisted. Closing the file on his desk, he stood up. 'That's all. I won't keep you.'

Although she had to dispel any suspicion that she would have liked to prolong the interview, Laurel could not leave without saying, 'Thank you for the car. When you said you'd do something about it, I thought you meant have the mechanics look it over. I never expected——'

'The job you do requires a reliable motor.' Trent's swift, almost curt interruption made her feel her thanks had been too fulsome. The car, like the meal, was a matter of business, not a personal gift from him to her.

'Of course,' she said quickly. She glanced back over her shoulder as she left the office, but he was already deep in something else.

During the next few weeks, Laurel did her utmost to present a calm, unemotional, businesslike front whenever she came into contact with Trent. It wasn't always easy. The magnetic pull of his attraction was such that if he was in a room her eyes were drawn to him, and she had to force herself to meet his gaze only when she was being spoken to.

She had never been this physically attracted to a man before, and found it hard to handle the sensations it produced in her, let alone do a competent job of hiding the

fact that he affected her at all. Her only real weapon
was a forced, deliberate coolness which she was afraid
made her sound brusque and impolite—the last thing
she wanted.

Why couldn't she be normal around him, she
lamented, as she was with Alan or Robin or any of the
other men she had to talk to and deal with every day?

Answer—because none of them made her feel the way
he did. She wanted him to look at her and smile that
slow, special smile she had not seen on his face for some
time. She wanted him to touch her, to feel his hands and
his mouth and—oh, God knew what she wanted!

Laurel buried her flaming face in her hands and consciously drove away the fantasies that always stopped at
a crucial point . . . because she dared not let them go
further. She did not know what making love fully felt
like, could only imagine, and was afraid to let her imagination take off, with Trent as its object, or one day
he might look into her eyes and know what she had been
thinking.

As it was, he returned her coolness with imper-
turbable formality, and it seemed to Laurel that the close
accord they had so briefly achieved when she worked
with him on the reports had been only a transient, passing
moment, gone and unrepeatable.

Of course, he had needed her then, she thought bitterly, so he had turned on his formidable charm to ex-
tract the best from her. And she had had her thanks: a
meal and a new car. He had no desire for her personal
friendship, and did not intend to give her his.

Easter was early that year, and the weather turned
suddenly and unexpectedly warm. Beneath the fresh
green of the Downs, the old houses of Lewes were soft,
mellowed grey stone and pastel-washed Georgian

façades. Daffodils nodded in the gardens and forsythia dripped golden over fences. A long, lazy Bank Holiday weekend lay ahead, and people looked forward to doing summer things—mowing the grass, walking along the breezy sea-front at Brighton, driving out into the countryside in the lengthening evenings.

'Any plans for the holiday weekend?' Laurel asked Clive hopefully, thinking that perhaps he would go away to stay with friends, or buzz up to London for a few days. But he shook his head dolefully.

'I'm penniless, Laurel my love,' he intoned mournfully.

'I could give you a loan—until you find a job,' she suggested, thinking it was at least a good sign that he wasn't dipping into the capital that his parents had left him.

'Trying to get rid of me?' he enquired from beneath raised eyebrows. 'Got plans that include having the house to yourself?'

'Don't be ridiculous!' she said scathingly.

'Silly me!' he cried, slapping his knee. 'Of course, lover-boy has his own pad! I'm surprised he hasn't taken over the Brighton Pavilion and gone in for high jinks, as the Prince Regent used to do.'

Laurel merely shrugged her shoulders disdainfully and refused to rise to the bait. Whatever Trent was, he wasn't a playboy hell-raiser. Most evenings he was still in the office when his management team went home, and according to Gloria invariably took work home with him.

'Not always Caterplus stuff. He's planning ahead for future projects, and his father keeps him heavily in- volved in what's going on in the US,' she had informed Laurel. 'I don't see where he fits in any private life,

although he gets lots of dinner invitations—and he's
joined the local gliding club.'

The same source indicated that Trent was living in a
rented apartment in Palmeira Square, a large, elegant
Georgian square built around gardens and overlooking
the Brighton sea-front.

'The rents are astronomical, but I suppose that's no
problem to him,' she said. 'The fact that he hasn't bought
a property must mean that he'll eventually move on else-
where—a pity. I've come to enjoy working for him. But
Castleford's European aspirations don't end here.'

Of course, Laurel told herself, she had known that all
along. Trent's elevated position in Castleford Industries
meant that he would not stay MD of one company longer
than it took to get it into line with the organisation. Then
he would be off, supervising the take-over of similar
companies all over Europe.

It was odd, but significant, that whereas a couple of
months earlier she would have been wondering gloomily
who they would send to occupy that position perma-
nently, now she was thinking, he'll leave, sooner or later,
and I won't see him again. Truly ships that passed in
the night.

And here was Clive, working himself up into a lather,
imagining that she and Trent were locked in a mad affair.
It had been difficult at home when all she had to do was
calmly but firmly maintain a distance between them, but
now Clive had it firmly fixed into his head that Laurel,
although refusing any involvement with him, was happily
giving herself to another man, she felt his jealous resentment growing with the passage of time. They were
no longer the boy and girl who had grown up together,
laughing and squabbling. He was an adult male, alone
in a house with a girl who would not play his game, and

he had nothing to do but brood on the unfairness of the situation—as he saw it—and live out fantasies similar to the ones about Trent that troubled her own reveries.

All the time she could feel the tension growing, and it finally came to a head on the Thursday night preceding Good Friday.

Laurel had come home to find the kitchen in a reasonable state, if only because it was one of Mrs Harvey's days for cleaning. Nothing had been done towards dinner, but, wanting to avoid friction at all costs, Laurel took frozen bolognese sauce from the freezer and improvised it into a passable lasagne, with salad, which she served at the pine table in the kitchen.

'Do we have to eat in here, like peasants?' Clive complained. 'We do have a perfectly good dining-room. Ana always lays the table properly, with good china and candles and a bottle of wine.'

'I've been working all day, and I can't be bothered,' said Laurel. 'If you'd wanted the dining-room table laid, why didn't you do it? You should be thankful I've cooked.'

'Yes, ma'am, thank you, ma'am.' He touched his forelock ingratiatingly. 'God, you're getting smug, Laurel! And bossy. Well, I'm going to have the wine, anyhow.'

He took a bottle of Côtes de Languedoc from the wine rack and uncorked it, and without worrying about niceties such as letting it breathe, slurped out two full glasses. At first, Laurel had intended to decline, but she reconsidered, thinking that he would drink the whole bottle himself and be quite impossible to deal with. As it was, his mood seemed to become more surly and unpleasant as the meal progressed, and as she was loading up the dishwasher she saw him reach for another bottle from the wine rack.

'Surely not——' she began, and suddenly Clive set the bottle on the table, his eyes narrowing, and turned on her, pinning her in the corner angle formed by the cupboard units.

'C'mon Laurel, loosen up. It's me, Clive, your childhood sweetheart,' he said, his voice slurring a little. 'Have a couple more glasses, and you'll feel nice and relaxed——'

His body trapped her against the cupboard, and feeling his strength, she knew the beginning of real fear.

'We were never childhood sweethearts, and we'll stop being friends unless you cut out this nonsense,' she said as calmly as she could.

'Good. Don't want to be friends,' he said truculently, and she wondered how many cans of lager he had consumed while watching TV all afternoon. He nuzzled her neck, and suddenly his hands grasped her breasts, hard and painfully, kneading and squeezing.

'You let *him* do this—why not me?' he demanded, and now Laurel knew he was beyond controlling or placating with words, and she had to get out—fast. She kneed him sharply in the groin, and while he was still cursing, and his grip relaxed, she wriggled free and made a dash down the corridor to the front door.

She ran all the way down the drive, along the road, until, quite sure he had not pursued her, she slowed to a fast walk, breathing heavily, her sides aching. Without thinking where she was going, she had come to the banks of the river that wound slowly through the town, and she sank down on to one of the wooden benches alongside the path, taking long, deep breaths and trying to recover herself.

There were few people about—a young couple strolled past, arms wrapped round each other's waists, a man walking his dog. Across the river, the broken outline of the castle ruins was dark against the deepening twilight. She sighed, letting her head droop forward, her shoulders slump, thinking I can't go home. I can't!

'Laurel?'

His voice cut through her despair, awakening her re-actions despite herself, and she twisted round on her seat to see Trent standing behind her. He was wearing casual fawn trousers and a soft brown sweater under a short, windcheater-type jacket, the first time she had ever seen him out of a suit.

'Trent...what...what are you doing here?' she asked faintly, thinking that with all her present problems she could not cope with this man's overpowering presence too.

'Killing time,' he said. 'I've just wound up at the office, and I'm catching the ten-thirty ferry to Dieppe.'

'Oh. You're going away for the weekend?' Laurel strove to keep her voice calm and normal, but her hands were shaking, and she clasped them tightly to keep them still. He looked at her more closely, and she knew she had not fooled him.

'Laurel, what's wrong? Are you in some sort of trouble?'

She bit her lip, shook her head, but he saw that two distraught tears were rolling down her cheeks, and she couldn't speak. Swifter than thought he was round the bench and seated beside her, his arm encircling her trembling shoulders.

'OK, Laurel, it's all right.' He spoke soothingly, quietly. 'Look—here's a handkerchief. Blow. Good girl!' He wiped the tears gently from her face and smiled into her eyes. 'There. You can tell me about it if you like. But you don't have to.'

She gazed at him beseechingly. For what seemed a long time she had been torn between fear of him and attraction, hardly able to think straight in his presence, desperate for his approval, resentful of his power. Now here he was, strong and unhesitant and certain of all he did, and unthinkingly she reached out to him in her need.

'I had an...an argument with Clive,' she half sobbed. 'I...I can't face him! I can't go home and I...I don't know what to do!'

Trent nodded thoughtfully.

'Clive. That's your...young man. The one who came to the office that day?'

'Yes. But he's not——' Laurel was too distracted, now, to begin to explain the complexities of her relationship to Clive. 'I think he's drunk—or getting that way. I don't know what he's going to do.'

Trent was silent for only a few moments. Then he said, 'Right, I'll tell you what we're going to do. I'll take you home—no——' as she started visibly '—listen to me, Laurel. You can pack a few things and come with me to Normandy. You've got a passport, I assume?'

She nodded. 'Yes, but...'

'No buts,' he insisted firmly. 'You don't have to worry—it will all be perfectly proper. I'll phone ahead to the hotel and reserve you a room. By the time you get back, after a few days away, it may all have blown over. If not—well, we'll see.'

Her first instinctive reaction had been, no, I can't do this. But that was quickly superseded by a feeling of intense relief that she didn't *have* to spend the weekend in the house with Clive, with whom she no longer felt safe, and it was as if a heavy weight flew from her

shoulders. She did not protest when Trent helped her to
her feet, nor did she remove her hand from the crook
of his arm as they walked along to where he had parked
the car while he stopped for a brief stroll by the river.
She felt warm and protected, as she had not felt for a
long time, safe behind the bulwark of this man's strength
and authority.

When they pulled up outside the house, all was in
darkness. It had still been daylight when Laurel had fled,
but for some reason Clive had failed to switch on the
lights when night began to fall. Laurel tensed as Trent
switched off the engine.

'If you wait for me here, I'll only be a few minutes,'
she said bravely, not wanting him to know how reluctant
she was to go inside.

'Not a chance,' he said cheerfully, getting out of the
car and preceding her up the drive. 'From what you
say...or rather, from what you *haven't* said...your friend
might be violent. Let me have your key.'

She gave it to him without demur, and he unlocked
the door and stepped into the hall, his body shielding
hers. 'Switch the light on, Laurel,' he said quietly, with
a glimmer of humour. 'Somehow I don't think he'll be
in a state to cause problems.'

Through the open door to the lounge, Laurel saw
Clive's inert body stretched out on the sofa. Trent walked
over and looked down at him, and Laurel asked ner-
vously, 'Is he all right?'

'He's fine,' he replied with a grim laugh. 'He won't
be feeling too terrific tomorrow, but that's his problem.
Go pack your stuff. We have to be at Newhaven an
hour before sailing. Meanwhile, if I can use your
phone——'

Laurel packed so quickly and in such a daze that she had no idea what was in her suitcase until she opened it at the other end. Her mind blanked, refusing to let her think too hard about what she was doing; she simply obeyed, like a programmed robot. At the last minute she wrote a short scrap of a note telling Clive she would be away for a few days, and left it in his room. Then she went downstairs to where Trent was calmly waiting in the hall, and allowed him to switch off the light, lock up, and lead her out to the car.

'I checked with the hotel,' he said, 'and I left a message on my answering machine at the office telling Gloria you wouldn't be in tomorrow.'

And she can make what she likes of that, Laurel thought numbly, as the car turned under the Cuilfail tunnel and on its way to Newhaven.

She was still numb as they drove on to the car deck in the bowels of the ship, locked the car and made their way up the flights of stairs to the passenger decks. Only as she stood at the rails watching as the port slipped away in the wake of the brightly lit ferry, and the darkness of the open sea closed around them, did Laurel turn to the man at her side and come alive with incredulity.

What in heaven's name am I doing? I'm going away with Trent Castleford! I must be insane!

Not that she feared she had jumped from the frying pan to the fire, nothing so simple. Trent had merely taken pity on her in her distraught state. He had booked her a separate room at the hotel, and she did not flatter herself he had any ideas of seducing her.

Right now, still smarting from the unpleasantness of Clive's assault, seduction was the last thing on Laurel's mind. But she had committed herself to several days away, alone, in Trent's company, and once the shock of what had happened wore off she knew that fierce attraction would flare anew in her. And she would have to conceal it from him. She would have to pretend that all she felt towards him was gratitude for his friendly gesture.

She honestly did not know how long she could maintain that deception in these relaxed, away-from-the-office circumstances, or if her performance would be good enough to fool him. She sighed heavily.

'Leave it behind you for the moment, Laurel,' he said, misinterpreting her anxiety. 'All relationships have ups and downs. It's getting chilly out here. Let's go to the bar and have a drink.'

They sat on vast green leather couches nursing glasses of brandy and looking out at the black, slightly choppy sea, the troughs of the waves silvered by furrows of moonlight, the caps white as ice.

'Since you've come along, you can help me with a rather pleasant task,' said Trent. 'The reason for this trip is that I'm planning on buying a property in Normandy. You can give me your opinion on the ones the estate agent has lined up for me to view.'

Laurel's dark eyes widened.

'Are you thinking of living there?'

'Not exactly. I shall be moving around Europe quite a lot in the next few years, but it will be somewhere to spend weekends when I'm close enough, and to relax whenever I get a little time to spare. I want something old enough to have character, but not falling to bits. Whereas I don't mind tarting it up as a form of relaxation therapy, I don't want builders living with me. And I must have somewhere with a bit of land.'

'You never cease to amaze me,' she said. 'I had you figured for a city type.'

He laughed.

'I was three years in Australia with various Castleford enterprises before coming to Europe this winter,' he told her. 'Most of my breaks were spent in the bush. You haven't got me figured at all, Laurel. I don't think you've got to first base yet.'

Laurel closed her hands around her glass and took a long sip of the brandy, hoping its warmth would dispel the sudden chill of apprehension around her heart. He was right. She didn't know him, for all he attracted her so strongly. Every guess she made turned out to be only half right, every move he made was not the one she expected of him. Why was she here with him now? Because he felt sorry for her? Or, who knew, because he was playing some other devious game, the rules of which she did not know?

In a mood of sudden restlessness, she downed the rest of her drink in one gulp. Well, the ship had already sailed, she thought. It was a long swim back to Newhaven, and she never did make more than the hundred metres front crawl! For whatever reasons, and whatever happened, she was here, and there was no going back now.

After finishing their drinks, they took a final turn round the moonlit decks before stretching out on the reclining seats in the quiet areas reserved for sleeping. Laurel closed her eyes. She could hear Trent's even, quiet breathing, inches away from her, imagine his long, lean elegant body relaxed in sleep. I won't be able to doze for even a minute, she thought, gripped by the febrile excitement the onset of school holidays had induced in her long ago.

The next thing she knew, a hand was shaking her shoulder, and she struggled blearily to gaze into Trent's face, clear-eyed, wide awake, radiating hard, clean masculinity.

'It's still dark!' she muttered.

'Of course it is. It's not three o'clock. But the ship will be docking at Dieppe soon. We've just time for coffee and croissants.'

How does he do it, on less than three hours' sleep? she wondered a little crossly. But later, as she sat in the car watching the bow doors open to the fresh spring air, and heard the engines revving as the queue of motorists prepared to drive off, her spirits reasserted themselves.

'Vive la France!' she grinned cheerfully.

Trent looked sidelong at her, and in the light from the dashboard his tawny eyes gleamed wickedly.

'I prefer "Who dares wins",' he said mysteriously as they drove out into the early morning stillness of the French port.

CHAPTER SEVEN

IT WAS still dark as they drove through the ancient city of Rouen where Joan of Arc had been burned at the stake centuries ago. But as they motored south a bluish tinge in the heavens presaged the dawn, and then the peaceful Norman countryside began to lighten and take shape all around them.

Cream and brown dappled cows munched the thick grass in verdant meadows fringed by orchards already starry with early blossom, sheep bleated in fields behind timbered farmhouses. Small villages awoke slowly as they passed through, a man in overalls cycled to work, cigarette dangling from his lips, women came back from the *boulangerie* with the first crusty baguettes of the day.

By the time they arrived in the pleasant, busy little town where Trent had booked the hotel, traders were setting up market stalls in the square, and were laying out huge round cheeses, blocks of rich butter, plump tomatoes and shiny apples and piles of dark, spicy sausages.

The hotel, which fronted on to the square, was not at all what Laurel had imagined J.J. Castleford's son to have chosen. It was a comfortably unpretentious *logis* without a hint of chrome or plate-glass luxury. A smiling middle-aged woman showed them their rooms, which were full of old-fashioned furniture—vast, dark oak wardrobes and huge beds with formidable bolsters and minimal pillows. Both rooms looked out over cool gardens and a river beyond, so the bustle in the square would not disturb them.

'I'm going to shower and then hit the sack until lunchtime,' Trent said practically. 'Three hours on one of those reclining seats isn't my idea of a night's sleep. I've no appointments to view until this afternoon, and I want my wits about me.'

Laurel thought she had never seen him with his wits less than razor-sharp, but she appreciated the logic of his words. And it was indicative of the strain under which she had been living for some time that, having showered and unpacked, she collapsed on to the enormous, comfortable bed and slept soundly and blissfully for several hours.

When she woke, sunlight was streaming through the window and birds were making a furious racket in the garden outside. She lay for a while, her mind blank, oddly contented, simply letting herself *be*. It was a release of which she had been long deprived, and she felt strength and confidence and a zest for living seeping back into her mind and body.

She had been lying thus for several peaceful minutes when Trent tapped lightly on her door and called, 'Laurel, are you awake?'

She slid her feet to the floor, crossed the room and opened the door to find him standing there, casually immaculate, ready to apply the same zeal and thoroughness to the purchase of his French property as he did to all his business dealings.

'It's twelve o'clock. Let's have an early lunch and go house-hunting,' he said.

Laurel instantly felt tousled and untidy, and her hand flew instinctively to her ruffled dark locks.

'All right. I'll give you five minutes to comb your hair and put on lipstick, and whatever you women do,' he said lightly, with an amused smile. 'I'll see you downstairs in the dining-room.'

The dining-room was more dark oak, starched napery and heavy silver plate cutlery. Outside, the river sparkled in the sun and two small dogs dozed on the grass, tails twitching occasionally in mysterious, rabbit-chasing dreams.

'We should jump in the deep end of Norman cuisine and have *tripes à la mode de Caen*,' Trent grinned, 'but I have to admit, ox-stomach doesn't appeal to me, whatever it's cooked in.'

'Ugh, me neither!' Laurel agreed, and after consideration they settled on *sole Dieppoise*, poached in cider with butter, salt and black pepper, served with prawns and mussels in the velvety cream sauce which was one of the glories of Norman cooking. After that, Laurel declared she had only room for the lightest apple soufflé, delicately flavoured with Calvados.

'Or I shall go home as fat as a pig!' she laughed, and Trent shook his head goodhumouredly.

'You're always worrying about your figure. From what I can see, your flesh is nicely distributed in all the right places,' he said, and for a moment his eyes lingered on her in a manner that made her feel suddenly weak and confused—as if he would have liked to touch those places, slowly and caressingly. What would it feel like, she wondered faintly, to be touched by him in that way— not just the swift but exciting embraces they had previously shared, but a long, leisurely lovemaking?

She took a sip of her coffee to calm these fevered images, but it was so hot it made her cough and brought tears to her eyes.

'I see I've embarrassed you,' he said, smiling just a little. 'It takes a mature woman to accept a compliment with aplomb. You're so sharp and bright; I keep forgetting how young you are.'

Laurel bristled.

'I'm twenty-one!' she said indignantly.

'I'm thirty-two. But it seems a lot longer than eleven years ago that I was your age,' he said.

'And I suppose you too mistakenly thought you had reached the heights of maturity, Grandad?' she demanded sarcastically, piqued by the way he had looked at her as if she were a woman, then proceeded to talk as if she were an innocent adolescent.

'I suppose I did,' he agreed. 'But in a way, I had more reason for that belief. I was living in a foreign country, surviving in a language and a currency strange to me. In addition to which, I was also married.'

Laurel gasped, and he subjected her to a look of knowing disbelief.

'Surely you're not going to pretend you didn't know I'd been married?' he said probingly, and she affected a shrug. Her surprise had not been the information, but the casual way he had suddenly imparted it. He was usually as tight as a clam about anything pertaining to his personal life.

'You won't drop anyone in it by admitting that you know,' he said gently. 'In a tight corner, Laurel, I'd certainly be glad to have you on my side. You're capable of great affection and staunch faithfulness towards your friends.'

'Isn't everyone?' she hedged, flustered.

'No, not everyone,' he stated flatly. 'Some are too wrapped up with number one, too self-obsessed to consider putting others first. Cara, my former wife, was like that—utterly self-absorbed—but, as I suppose you also know, she's a singer, and perhaps all truly great artists are blessed—or cursed—by that kind of tunnel vision.'

He spoke lightly, but did not quite succeed in tamping down the undertone of regret in his voice. Laurel knew, in that moment, beyond doubt, that this woman had hurt him badly; she suspected that he was still not completely over her, and perhaps never would be.

She abandoned her pretence of ignorance—after all, he was aware that she had heard the various snippets of gossip about his life.

'Is she ... your ex-wife ... is she very talented?'

Trent met her eyes soberly.

'You could say that. History will probably put her up there with the likes of Callas and Melba,' he said, his voice factual and unexaggerated. 'It's that vital, incalculable difference, as I told you once before, between being good and being great. Cara is great. She has it.'

'That must have been ... very difficult for you, when you were married to her,' Laurel hazarded, but he shook his head.

'That wasn't the reason we split up. I could have handled Cara's success, her brilliance. I rejoiced in it for her. If she'd still had time for our marriage, I believe we could have made it. It was all very fine while we were both students together, but later, it got so that nothing else mattered. *Her* voice, *her* career, always *her*. I couldn't sit around waiting for any woman's favours,' he said savagely. 'We finally separated six years ago, after five years of marriage, although during the last couple our paths didn't cross very much.'

'Do you ever see her now?' Laurel asked. The answer was strangely important to her, and yet the reply was unsatisfactory, not telling her what she really wanted to know—the continuing level of his involvement.

'Occasionally, when she happens to be singing anywhere I also happen to be,' he said with a grimace. Then he shook his head, as if surprised at himself. 'I don't know why I'm telling you all this, Laurel. I don't talk about it as a rule.'

Because it disturbed painful memories he still could not bear to examine too closely?

'Nothing you have told me will go any further,' she promised.

'I know that,' he said. 'I'd stake my reputation on it.'

And then, having opened the door and allowed her a peep inside, he closed it again firmly.

'Are you ready? We have to meet the real estate man in fifteen minutes' time.'

Guillaume Grouet, the estate agent, was a dapper man with a likeable smile. He and Trent had not previously met, but had obviously conversed at length on the phone. He knew what his influential client was looking for, and had a list drawn up of properties he considered worth viewing.

Trent introduced Laurel simply as 'my colleague, Miss Ashby', which seemed to state that she would not be sharing the house with him and her personal approval was therefore not essential. But Guillaume Grouet was French and took this with a pinch of salt, Laurel thought, amused and slightly embarrassed each time he turned to her and asked smilingly, 'Don't you think so, *mademoiselle*?' or, 'Charming, is it not, *hein*?'

By four o'clock they had seen a number of cottages and Trent had remained non-committal about all of them, although, as Laurel well knew, that might not necessarily mean he wasn't interested.

The final property they saw was a mile or so outside a tiny village, and tucked away along a meandering little lane. The walls were cream and brown half-timbered, the garden was waist-high in grass and weeds, and it was obvious no one had lived here for many years. Inside, there was a large living-room with a huge fireplace and a kitchen which looked as if it had not been updated since before World War One. Upstairs, three bedrooms and a rusty, antiquated shower-room.

'It's been badly neglected,' said Guillaume, with a dismissive shrug, brushing the clinging dust from his suit jacket. 'Really, I don't know why I included it on the list. It's in a poor state decoratively, as you can see.'

'It certainly is,' Trent agreed unrevealingly. Apparently casually, he laid a hand on Laurel's shoulder, and a fierce tremor ran along her arm at his touch. Then she realised that he was covertly drawing her attention to the window, and looking out, she saw, beyond the overgrown garden, a little stream gurgling through an orchard of gnarled, ancient fruit trees.

In her mind, she cut the grass, cleared the weeds and made a rustic bridge over the stream, put chairs and a table beneath the trees. It could be quite idyllic, she thought, and, turning towards Trent, she almost blurted out her thoughts, convinced that he shared them.

Then she remembered that one didn't let agents know the extent of one's interest in a property. Although Trent could well afford the asking price of this house, he would get the best deal he could, none the less, because that was how he had learned business at his father's knee. Laurel bit back her words of praise and tried to keep her too-revealing dark eyes deliberately blank.

'I reckon we've seen enough for today,' said Trent. 'Perhaps we could continue tomorrow.'

'*D'accord,*' Guillaume agreed. He got into his car, and Trent and Laurel set off in theirs. But Trent only drove a hundred yards before turning back to the house, and getting out, he took Laurel's hand and led her through the long grass to the orchard, from where they stood, looking back.

'It's perfect,' he said. 'OK, inside needs quite a lot of attention, and the creature comforts require updating, but the walls and the roof look structurally sound. And this garden, Laurel, is exactly right.'

'It's lovely,' she agreed wistfully. 'I thought so the minute I looked out of the upstairs window. I'm afraid I almost gave the game away to Monsieur Grouet.'

He laughed.

'So you did. Those eyes could never hide anything—they weren't designed to,' he said, and touched the tip of her nose with his finger. Laurel found she was holding her breath quite painfully, believing that he was going to kiss her. *Wanting* him to kiss her. Then he appeared to take a step back mentally.

'I'll play the game, and let Grouet show us the rest of the properties on his list tomorrow,' he said. 'Then I'll put in an offer.'

Laurel turned away and pretended to look down into the clear depths of the stream. She was knotted up inside with unsatisfied longings, still straining towards the kisses he had not given her. Why did he do this to her, tantalising her with the occasional touch, meaningful looks and those oblique comments, if he had no desire for her? She found it hard to believe he was totally unaware of the effect he had on her, however hard she had tried to hide it. His perceptions were too acute for that. Did he want her, or was he merely amusing himself?

That evening, Trent suggested they eat out somewhere else instead of dining at the hotel, much as they had enjoyed their lunch. Laurel had confessed that she had never been further into Normandy than a day trip to Dieppe, and he viewed this with incredulity.

'Amazing—you've lived all your life just the other side of the Channel and never got around to exploring what's virtually on your doorstep,' he castigated her. 'You really must see something of the coast and countryside.'

Laurel had packed so haphazardly that she found it difficult to select a suitable, co-ordinated outfit for an evening out. But she did have a good black linen jacket she had snatched off the peg as she left home, and a fairly smart white skirt. A frantic fifteen minutes searching for something to wear under the jacket produced a peach and white printed top with a lacy shawl collar, then she brushed her hair back behind her ears and fixed on large gold hoop earrings.

So why the fuss? she asked herself. What am I trying to do, or to prove? She hastily excused herself on the grounds that any woman going out for dinner naturally wanted to look her best, in any circumstances.

But she knew that was not really the answer. She had dressed up with great care because she was going out for the evening with a man to whom she was deeply attracted, who insisted on giving her conflicting signals as to how he felt about her. In some oblique way, she knew, she was trying to make him reveal his hand.

They drove through the luxuriant countryside to the intensely picturesque small port of Honfleur, where colourful boats were moored in the basin of the Lieutenance, its harbour, and tall old houses reflected themselves in the water. The quay was lively with strollers, bright with cafés and restaurants, and they sat at an outside table beneath an awning, watching the marine activity and the passers-by while they drank pastis and ate their first course—*moules marinière*, tiny mussels in their shiny black shells cooked in white wine, shallots and parsley.

'You're looking a whole lot better than you did twenty-four hours ago, Laurel,' Trent smiled softly, filling her glass with crisp Muscadet to accompany the *faisan à la cauchoise*—pheasant in a Calvados sauce served with sweet, fried apples. 'I have to say this for you—you don't let romantic problems interfere with your appetite.'

Laurel frowned, her dark eyes flickering puzzlement, and then she quivered inwardly with sudden mortification. Was he implying that her feelings for him were so obviously overpowering she might reasonably be expected to be off her food? Surely she had not given herself away to that extent? She had tried her hardest to behave in a calm, friendly, normal manner.

'I haven't any romantic problems,' she declared firmly.

His golden-brown eyebrows rose reprovingly. 'Oh, Laurel, you don't have to pretend to me,' he said. 'All that fracas with your young man yesterday. It seems to me you *do* have problems, although perhaps "romantic" isn't the most appropriate word. If you asked my advice, I'd say a woman is better off without a man who might be violent under the influence of drink.'

Laurel sighed heavily. She was going to have to clear up this misapprehension which had its roots in their earliest meetings, whatever it cost her in face.

'Clive isn't my "young man", Trent,' she told him soberly. 'I should have made that clear yesterday, if I hadn't before.'

His eyes narrowed to tawny slits as he said, 'But he's living at your house, in your parents' absence. You can't expect me to believe that you're no more than friends?'

Of course that was how it must have appeared, given that she had not levelled with him earlier about her relationship with Clive! He thought she was having a private fling while Robert and Ana were away, and things had got out of hand! Laurel stifled a groan, and her cheeks flamed.

'He always lives there when he's in Lewes,' she explained. 'It's his home. Clive is Robert's nephew. He and I grew up together, although, as I was adopted, we're not actually related.'

Amused understanding glinted in his eyes as he digested her confession.

'And I always thought he was your boyfriend, ever since I saw you together at the Golf Club,' he said, with a knowing grin which made her blush all the more at her own deception. 'You didn't disabuse me of that belief, did you, Laurel? One might say you passively allowed me to continue in it. Now I wonder why you should choose to do that?'

'It wasn't any of your business until yesterday,' she retorted swiftly. 'I wasn't under any obligation to explain my personal life to you, any more than you had to tell me about your marriage.' She paused, well aware that this was not an apt comparison. He might have said nothing about Cara until today, but he had not gone out of his way deliberately to mislead her. Clearing her throat, she stumbled on, 'Having...involved you in my problems, I...well, I feel I owe you an explanation.'

His fingers steepled together, Trent rested his chin on them and looked at her closely, penetratingly, his eyes reflecting the glow of the lamp the waiter had just lit on their table.

'So explain. What exactly did happen yesterday to send you rushing out of the house in such a state?' he demanded. 'It certainly wasn't an everyday argument. Nor do I get the impression that this is a brother-sister relationship, despite what you say.'

'But it is, so far as I'm concerned,' she insisted. 'The trouble is that lately, Clive seems to have…to have other ideas. And last night, he…well, he just got too persistent. He tried to…' She looked down, suddenly ashamed, though she didn't know why, since she had been the victim, not the culprit, and she had not invited those unpleasant drunken advances.

'All right, Laurel, I get the idea,' Trent said quietly. 'There's no need to expound any further. But we're going to have to think hard about what you're going to do when you get home. You can't share a house with a man who's liable to attack you. OK, it may never happen again, but the strain on you would be far too great.'

It was all most odd. So short a time ago, his decisive 'we're going to have to think hard about what you're going to do' would have made her bristle with indignation. 'I'll take care of myself,' would have been her immediate and automatic reaction. But now, his protectiveness made her glow with an unaccustomed warmth, making her feel that he must in some way care about her to show such concern.

Her gaze moved upwards from the tanned throat visible above his open-necked shirt, to the strong, arresting mouth and those hypnotic eyes which now held hers above the glass he raised to her.

'I think I know why you allowed me to go on believing you were involved with Clive,' he said.

'You do?' Her voice was scarcely more than a whisper croaked out from a throat suddenly dry.

He set down his glass and took her hand; upturning the palm, he rubbed his thumb over the spot where it joined her wrist, above a delicate tracery of veins.

'It was a way of holding me at arm's length,' he said softly. 'You knew—you must have known—I was attracted to you, from the first day we met. I was sure you felt the same, even when you resented me for taking over Caterplus. I couldn't have imagined that current that flowed between us.'

The light, tantalising touch of his hand sent ripples of sensation coursing along her arm, and she closed her eyes briefly.

'I felt it . . . but I didn't know where I was, with you,' she said, in the same scarcely audible voice. 'I thought you found me attractive . . . and then you behaved as though you weren't remotely interested.'

'Because I don't mess with other guys' women,' he explained. 'At least, I try not to, although there were occasions when it was hard to keep my hands off you. Are you afraid of me, Laurel?'

'A little,' she admitted honestly.

He laughed, a low, sensuous chuckle.

'That's one of the things I like best about you—the way you aren't ashamed to admit your doubts and apprehensions,' he said. 'Of course, there are other things I like. Your eyes—they're full of invitations you don't even know you're giving. Your mouth—the way you bite your lower lip when you're anxious or angry. Your——'

'Trent, stop!' she exclaimed, in a frenzy of confused reactions, all her senses racing in different directions and colliding headlong. To have been observed so minutely made it plain beyond doubt that he desired her, and she found herself stretched on a rack of delight and excitement, torn between desire and fear.

He said, 'I want to take you back to the hotel. Right now. And if I do, you know what's going to happen, don't you?'

She met his eyes directly.

'I know,' she whispered.

'If that's not what you want, Laurel, then say so now, because once I touch you....' He left the image unfinished, and she shivered. It was inevitable, fated, and had been since she had met him.

'It's what I want,' she said softly but clearly.

Trent signalled for the bill and left a handful of notes on the table, before wordlessly taking her hand and leading her back to the car.

During the drive back, Laurel sat at his side in a daze, trying not to think too hard about what would happen when they got to the hotel. Part of her was in a fever of impatience to feel his mouth and his hands on her, but in a deeper, more primitive recess of her psyche she was nervous and a little afraid, still holding back on the brink of this deep commitment.

The powerful maleness of him she had sensed at their first meeting both drew her on and scared her. He would be sensual, experienced, demanding, and she was all but ignorant, unsure of how to please, frightened of the unknown.

But it had to happen to her some time, she told herself as he collected both keys from reception and she walked upstairs at his side. And she wanted it to be with him— of that she was quite, quite sure.

Trent unlocked the door of her room, letting her precede him in, and quietly closed it behind them. It was dark outside now, but the curtains were undrawn and moonlight illuminated the room, silvering a path across the bed in readiness for them. Silently he shed his jacket, and she stood motionless as he came up behind her and slid hers from her shoulders.

She felt his mouth graze the nape of her neck, his hands lifting her hair first, then she shivered with delicious vulnerability as his fingers undid the buttons of her top, drew it aside and deftly peeled down her lacy underwear, exposing her breasts. Laurel cried out involuntarily, submitting to the piercing sensations of pleasure as his hands stroked and pinched and caressed, knowing she had been subconsciously waiting for and desiring this since that moment long ago at the inn.

'You were made for this, Laurel,' he murmured, lifting her up and carrying her to the bed. 'It will be the easiest and most pleasurable of lessons.'

He set her back on the pillows and his mouth found hers, teasing the silky skin of her inner lip, his tongue probing deliciously, so that her head spun and she scarcely knew or cared where she was. Pleasure followed pleasure as he kissed her breasts, shrugging out of his shirt so that of their own volition, her hands sought his naked back and searched a path up his spine.

He had gently eased off her skirt and was exploring the smooth skin of her legs, when a sudden burst of music drifted in through the slightly open window. Someone in one of the other rooms was listening to the radio, a man's and a woman's voice singing, and even the most musically uneducated would have recognised the melody, if they knew no other piece of operatic score. The love duet from *La Bohème*, Rodolfo and Mimi searching for her key by candlelight, and falling in love.

Trent stiffened briefly, imperceptibly, his hands stilled, his breath caught, for the merest, truant fraction of a heartbeat, yet Laurel, all her senses alive and vibrantly attuned to him, felt it nevertheless. And then he took her determinedly in his arms, kissing her with a hard, savage passion born of desperate need, a maturity of longing she had never yet known and could not yet match.

Fear rose up in her, rampant—fear of being engulfed by this fierce, powerful force of sexuality over which she had no control. Fear of giving herself utterly and without restraint to a man who, in some dark, inarticulate corner of her mind, she suspected was still painfully involved with another woman. She went rigid and unresponsive in his arms, her hands braced against his chest, her eyes wide, and for a moment they remained locked together thus, unmoving.

Then his hold slackened, he sighed, smiled ruefully and let her go altogether.

'All right, Laurel, relax,' he said quietly. 'I'm not going to force you to do anything against your will. I thought you were ready for this, but obviously you aren't, not really.'

Instinctively she pulled the quilt over her half-naked body, but he did not look at her as he buttoned on his shirt and picked up his jacket. The door clicked quietly as he closed it behind him, leaving her alone, racked with shame and confusion.

Too true, I'm not ready, she thought, burning with angry humiliation. Not ready to lose my virginity to a man who, in the moment before making love to me, is suddenly reminded of someone else. Someone he can't forget and from whom he isn't really free.

Cara, Cara—damn her! Cara, whom Laurel had never even met, who had the power to meddle in her life, to come between Laurel and the only man she had ever really wanted. Cara, she of the angelic voice, who reached out from their shared, bitter past to exert her inescapable pull over Trent, even as he held Laurel in his arms.

He wanted me, but right at that moment, when I would have been his, it was *her* he was thinking of, she reminded herself wretchedly. It wasn't enough.

She lay for a long time, nursing her own hurt, her own frustration, her own failure, as she saw it, before finally drifting into an angry, restless sleep.

In the middle of the night she awoke with a mind washed clean of the mists of self, and she thought, my God, poor Trent, how ghastly for him. To have been so hurt by a woman, and yet still to be so deeply in thrall to her that after so many years, on the verge of an intimate moment with someone else, her powerful image came back to haunt him. How awful for him—how utterly alone and desolate he must have felt!

And yet he had let her be, had not used his superior strength to overcome her, his persuasive charm to coax her back into his arms, as he might easily have done. The corporate piranha had proved himself to be a gentleman after all, and she, unappreciative of his restraint and insensitive to his sufferings, had not had the grace to be thankful for it!

Laurel learned a hard lesson that night. Trent himself had told her she was capable of fierce loyalty and affection towards those she cared for. She knew, now, that she was also capable of strong passion—the feelings he had aroused in her left her in no doubt of that.

But in the quiet loneliness of her room, wrapped in the stillness of darkened Normandy outside, she knew how it felt to think herself inside another person's skin, to understand that person's pain—to feel it, not quite as he felt it, but close enough. With this shedding of another layer of self, overnight, the girl she had been took a step towards the woman she was fast becoming. The woman that knowing Trent Castleford was helping to make her.

When morning finally came, Laurel gave herself no time for qualms or hesitations. Slipping into jeans and a striped rugby shirt, she knocked on the door of his room, which was next to hers.

There was no answer, so she went down to the dining-room where she found him already having breakfast.

He greeted her quite normally, without animosity or embarrassment, as if she hadn't been half naked in his arms the night before.

'I thought you might want to sleep in a while, so I didn't disturb you,' he said. 'We aren't due to meet Grouet until ten o'clock. In fact, you don't have to come along at all if you'd sooner shop, or sunbathe, or whatever.'

Distancing himself again already, she thought. He had made his move towards her, and she had proved unequal to it. Maybe he wouldn't think it worth the trouble of trying again.

'Trent.' Laurel slipped into the seat opposite him and spoke quickly, forcing the words out before she could change her mind and chicken out. 'I want you to know that I'm sorry about last night, and that I understand how you felt.'

His eyes, as he looked at her across the table, were remote and cool.

'Do you, Laurel?' he asked blankly. 'I would very seriously doubt it. Perhaps it was a mistake to bring you along at all. Certainly it was a misjudgement to try to make love to you. It won't happen again.'

CHAPTER EIGHT

IN THE END, she did go along with him to meet Guillaume Grouet, and they spent most of Saturday looking at properties—fruitlessly, Laurel knew, since Trent had already made up his mind.

Still, she was thankful for the presence of a third party, since the atmosphere between Trent and herself was as tense as it had ever been.

Not that he was unpleasant to her. On the contrary, he was polite and considerate, and so formal that Laurel could scarcely endure it, after they had come so close to being much, much more to one another.

She regretted now the fear and the unthinking jealousy that had made her pull away from him, and wished she had conquered both her resentment and her natural nervousness and allowed things to take their course.

An older, more experienced woman would have ignored his brief reaction to the music, and let him continue making love to her, trusting that once they were full and complete lovers her own image would be superimposed on that of the woman he was remembering. That was what I should have done if I really wanted him, Laurel thought wretchedly, instead of cutting up like a stupid, ignorant girl.

Things could have been so different this morning if she had. She could at least have kept his desire for her alive, so that she was the one on his mind, and maybe, who knew, little by little, Cara might have faded from his dreams.

She had tried once more to explain her feelings to him.

'Trent, it wasn't that I didn't want you to make love to me,' she said. 'It was simply that when——'

'Leave it, Laurel,' he said curtly, cutting her off in mid-sentence. 'I ought to have known better. You're too young for me, and I should have left well alone when I realised you were a virgin. There aren't too many of them around, at twenty-one.'

At this, her temper had finally flared.

'Well, I'm certainly not going to apologise for that!' she said proudly. 'I don't jump into bed with people all that lightly.'

'I know you don't. You made that quite clear,' he said drily. 'But Laurel, if you don't want to start a fire, don't strike the match!'

This was too much! He was all but implying that she was a tease, the sort of girl who took off her clothes and then shouted 'Rape!'

'Right. And when I'm really ready for a conflagration, I'll make sure I find a man who's single-mindedly intent on tending the blaze!' she retorted sarcastically.

'Flowers and champagne and a full orchestra playing in the background?' he asked mockingly. 'Good luck, Laurel, but there's usually something that gets in the way. It's called life.'

At that she had turned away disgustedly and refused to continue the conversation. He had not pursued it, and a frosty silence had fallen between them. As the day passed, it had eased slightly, until a constrained courtesy prevailed, and she accepted sadly that this was as good as it was going to get. They could not recapture the spellbinding chemistry that had gripped them both at the harbourside restaurant at Honfleur, and she wondered if they could even return to a working friendship. Too much—or too little—had happened, leaving their relationship in limbo, with nowhere to go.

Late on Saturday afternoon, Trent put in an offer for the cottage he had seen and liked the previous day, and Laurel was quite surprised when they immediately repaired to the local *notaire*'s office to sign a contract.

'It's quite usual in France to sign at this stage,' the estate agent told her. 'The preliminary contract is called a *compromis de vente*, and is, naturally, conditional upon any defects or limitations being discovered. It means we do not have all this—how do you call it— gazumping you have in England. Much less stressful!'

Trent read the contract carefully, asked several pertinent questions regarding it, and seemed to have grasped the fine points with his usual thoroughness.

'That certainly didn't take too long,' Laurel remarked as they drove back to the hotel, trying her best to lighten the atmosphere between them a little.

'When one has made up one's mind about something, there doesn't seem to be any sense in hanging about, or backtracking,' he said pointedly, and Laurel had to believe that this remark was slanted at her. But she bit her lip and refused to rise to it. There was nothing to be gained by going over the same ground again, and she was blowed if she would apologise further for only wanting a man whose heart and mind, not merely his body and his senses, were concentrated on her.

Dinner at the hotel that night was a mostly silent, sombre business, a matter simply of eating because it was necessary to do so. Trent, for all he had found and purchased the house he wanted, in no way appeared to be celebrating his success, and the holiday mood had evaporated. He wanted only to be back at his desk,

getting on with work which was waiting for him. And
he wanted to be free of her, Laurel had to surmise.

'We'll catch the first boat tomorrow,' he said. 'Can
you be ready early? There should be space, if we're at
Dieppe in plenty of time.'

Laurel indicated tersely that that would be fine by her,
as if she too would be only too glad to get back. As in
a way, she would. The situation had become impossible.
Yet she knew that never again, most likely, would she
be alone with Trent, and, painful as they were, these last
hours were meaningful for her. She had never known
she could be the victim of such fiercely contradictory
emotions, all at one and the same time!

They arrived back at Newhaven early on Sunday
afternoon, after a crossing Trent spent immersed in a
pile of newspapers he had bought in Dieppe, while Laurel
aimlessly prowled the decks, watching the French coast
disappear and waiting for a sight of the Sussex cliffs.
So much had changed for her, in so short a time, that
a different Laurel was going home.

Trent drove straight to her house without a word. Only
when they arrived, he said shortly, 'Right. Let's see how
the land lies.'

'There's no need for you to trouble yourself,' Laurel
said swiftly. 'I can cope, I'm sure.'

She might have basked in his protectiveness before,
taking it as a token of the way a man showed that he
cared for a woman, but now she objected strongly to it.
He didn't care—he only thought her incapable of looking after herself, and a responsibility he felt obliged to
discharge.

'Uh-uh. There's no way you're going in there on your
own,' he said firmly, and although she glared up at him

like a small, angry tigress he would not release her suitcase or give her back the key he held in his hand.

'Very well. But it's not necessary,' she said huffily, preceding him up the path. 'I can manage. After all, I've known Clive all my life.'

'What a short memory you have,' he said drily, unlocking the door, and Laurel had sufficient shame to look away, recalling how she had sat on the riverside bench sobbing, 'I can't go home!'

'OK, perhaps I over-reacted,' she muttered, following him into the house, into that weird stillness one only found when a place was empty and unlived-in.

There was a sealed envelope on the kitchen table, with her name on it in Clive's handwriting, and she opened it, conscious of Trent's watchful eyes on her as she read the note inside.

> Laurel, I'm sorry. I don't know what came over me. I must have had a brainstorm, and I can only blame the demon drink. I *have* been knocking back more than usual, lately.
>
> Anyhow I've gone over to stay with Johnny Willis near Uckfield for a while. You know—his old man owns the big garden centre just outside the town, and he's promised to give me a job.
>
> Uncle Robert phoned from Jamaica to say they'd be coming home before too long. See you soon. Meanwhile, take care. Clive.

The letter was so utterly normal, the writer sounded so much like the old Clive, the one she had always known, that Laurel blinked away tears of relief. Trent, still watching her, said nothing, but she could feel him waiting for her to explain.

'It's all right,' she told him crisply. 'Clive's gone away to stay with a friend. And my father and Ana are coming home soon. So you see, there's no reason for you to concern yourself over me.'

That sounded ungrateful, and she regretted the words as soon as they were out. His initial impulse in taking her with him had been for her own safety, and, far from having deviously planned to seduce her, Laurel knew that he had only reacted to the way things had developed spontaneously between them when he'd discovered that she and Clive were not lovers. But she could not snatch the words back, and his disdainful stare told her what a low opinion he had of her manners.

'In that case, I'll be on my way,' he said laconically, turning abruptly and striding briskly down the hall towards the front door.

The old wilful, girlish Laurel would have let him go without a word. The new, more considerate, more thoughtful Laurel still emerging from that chrysalis could not quite bear to say 'to hell with him', disregarding how glad she had once had reason to be of his strength and his decisive action.

She caught up with him halfway down the drive.

'Trent!'

He paused, turned and looked questioningly back at her, his eyes once again telling her absolutely nothing of the inner workings of his mind. He gave her no help, merely waited to hear whatever she had to say, and she moistened her lips and drew a deep breath, determined to do what was right, whether she liked it or not.

'I just wanted to say thank you. You got me out of an awkward situation, and I'm not unappreciative.'

'Even if I almost landed you in another one, equally awkward,' he said, with faint mockery. 'Forget it, Laurel.

It was an...interesting weekend. I dare say we'll both survive.'

Robert and Ana arrived back in England at the beginning of May, looking very tanned, as might have been expected, but neither of them was as relaxed and carefree as they should have been, after a long, leisurely cruise and a winter in the sun.

'So how was the Caribbean?' Laurel asked her father as they sat in the garden after dinner, a few nights after they arrived home. 'I've been waiting for lots of fabulous descriptions of all you saw, and so far neither of you has said very much.'

'Hot,' Robert said shortly. 'It was hot and sticky. I can't think why people go away to escape the English winter, only to endure a climate not natural to live in.'

Indeed, Laurel thought, he looked more tired than she had seen him look after a long, taxing day at Caterplus, as if all the energy and enthusiasm for living had drained out of him. She had heard that sometimes happened on retirement, and she herself had suspected it might happen in Robert's case, but somehow that easy answer no longer satisfied her entirely.

For one thing, he had not asked her how things were at work, how she was coping, how the new management was making out—things she would have expected him to be agog to know. When she tried tentatively to introduce the subject, he seemed apathetic, and she had the feeling he wasn't really listening to what she was saying.

But she would have kept her misgivings to herself, were it not for Ana. Ana was like a barometer where Robert was concerned. He was her whole life, and she was only happy when he was happy.

Laurel could see very plainly that Ana was not happy. She was restless and ill at ease, her hands fluttered and would not be still, her eyes anxiously followed her husband wherever he went.

'I get the feeling,' Laurel said gently to her stepmother one Sunday afternoon when they were alone, 'that the holiday was not an unqualified success. Correct me if I'm wrong.'

Ana sighed.

'No, you're not wrong, *cariña*. Your father did not like the heat, although truly, it was not that bad—very pleasant, in fact. He did not like the food. He found shipboard life tedious. He complained about the insects, about poor service, about——' She pushed a hand through the long dark hair just beginning to thread with grey. '*Dios*, I got so sick of hearing him complain, there were times when I felt I could hit him!'

Laurel frowned in puzzlement. This sounded more like a querulous, invalid octogenarian than the brisk, decisive man who had brought her up as his daughter and taught her much of what she knew.

'It's uncharacteristic,' she said. 'He was so looking forward to going away, just the two of you.'

'I know.' Ana lowered her voice, although Robert had retired to the room he still referred to as his study, where he had taken to spending a lot of his time. 'I wondered if he was quite well, but when I asked him he said he was perfectly all right, and told me not to be silly. But ...a wife knows these things, and I am not so sure. He seems to need more sleep, more rest, I tell him, than he ever has, all the years I have known him.'

'And what's his answer to that?' Laurel demanded worriedly.

'That he's getting older, and I should not expect him to behave like a twenty-year-old!' Ana made a moue of disgust. 'Then he makes joke and says perhaps I need a younger man, so I throw a cushion at him.'

Momentarily, Ana's wide, engaging smile lit her face, as it rarely had since they came home, and Laurel saw that the cruise had given her *some* happy memories. But she was anxious and not reassured, that much was plain to see.

'Perhaps I should talk to him—ask him outright if there's anything the matter,' Laurel mused, but Ana shook her head warningly.

'No, do not,' she begged forcefully. 'You will get no-where, I assure you. Perhaps all will be well now we are home, and the summer has come—well, what passes for summer in England,' she grimaced disparagingly. 'At least he will not be able to complain it is too hot!'

So Laurel kept silent, reminding herself that Robert was unlikely to tell her if anything was wrong and withhold the information from Ana. But she was troubled, for it seemed to her that, far from recovering from whatever malaise had gripped him on holiday, he was deteriorating very gradually, in ways not always easy to define, before her eyes.

There was no one with whom she could talk over her anxieties. Ana, after her initial confidences, seemed eager to believe that Robert was on the mend, and would soon be himself again.

She tried hinting to Clive that she was not altogether happy about her father, but that did not get her very far. He only replied that if Robert insisted he was all right, then undoubtedly that must be the case.

Clive was still staying with his friend near Uckfield, and working at the garden centre, but he had started coming over for occasional dinners and Sunday lunch, telling Ana that really it was easier for him to live at Johnny's, because of the early start to the working day. He looked fit and brown, and Laurel was pleased to learn that he appeared to enjoy the work. Johnny's father was thinking of handing the business over to his son, and there had been talk of Clive's going into partnership.

'That's great,' Laurel had enthused. 'I'm so glad you've found something you like, and if you do decide to become partners with Johnny you could sink some of the money your parents left you into the business.'

She and Clive were not quite the easy, casual friends they had once been, although matters were improving. He had phoned her a few days after she returned from Normandy to ask her if she would meet him somewhere for a drink and a chat, and on the neutral ground of a pub bar in Lewes, he had apologised for his behaviour. Nothing like that would ever, ever happen again, he had assured her, and please could they be friends, as he would hate to lose her.

Laurel could never bear a grudge for long, and since then they had gone out for a drink or a meal together a number of times, and he had behaved impeccably. His frenzied attack on her must, she decided, have been an aberration brought on by drink, boredom and enforced proximity. The only contact he ventured to risk, now, was a brief peck on the cheek when they said goodbye.

Nor did he interrogate her about Trent, although he must have guessed she had gone away with him.

'I'm not going to ask you anything about that man you work for,' he had declared when they first met again. 'It's none of my business, and I was well out of order. I accept that the subject is off limits.'

'Clive, it's not off limits at all, it's just that really there's nothing to get steamed up about,' she had replied wearily. 'I admit he attracted me, but it came to nothing very much. If there was ever anything between us, it's well over. I really would prefer not to talk about Trent Castleford, if it's all the same by you.'

'Fine by me,' he had said, with rather too much enthusiasm, adding quickly, 'That is—I thought you were out of your depth and might get hurt.'

And he wasn't far wrong there, Laurel had thought ruefully. She *had* got hurt. Furthermore, the hurt was only compounded by the cruel knowledge that since they had got back from Normandy, she might just as well have ceased to exist for Trent.

He spoke to her, of course, when he had to, and since she worked for him that was fairly frequently. But only as a colleague, and only when it was necessary. No one at Caterplus, not even the ever-watchful Gloria, would ever have guessed that once, in a hotel bedroom, she and Trent had come close to being lovers, that she had trembled in his arms and submitted passionately to his caresses. His manner towards her was so matter-of-fact, so calmly businesslike, one would have been hard pressed to discern whether he even liked her, as a person. Or thought of her as an individual at all.

She imagined their relationship as a tender shrub that had just been about to flower when some sort of blight had stricken it, and the blossom had failed to unfurl. He had been unprepared to nurture it along and give it a second chance. Refusing even to let it wither and fade of its own accord, he had taken a sharp pair of cutters and ruthlessly snapped off its head. But the roots were still there, suffering and deprived. Laurel could still not forget the joy of being with him, the delight of his touch, those few sunlit hours when the world had begun to open up before them, full of promise.

Drop it, Laurel. *He's* forgotten, she thought, looking across the desk at him on one of the weekly management meetings, and quickly looking away again before he saw the regret in her eyes.

Despite what Ana had said, May turned unusually hot, a stream of near-Mediterranean weather settled over the south of England, bringing people out in scanty clothes and the gardens in a riot of exaggerated colour.

At the top of the high street was a church whose burial ground was an oasis of peace. Its back turned on the traffic, it sloped gently down a hill, looking across at the green rise of the Downs. The graves were not set in orderly patterns, but haphazardly, among grass which was not always cut short, bushy shrubs and a profusion of wild flowers, moon daisies and marigolds, forget-me-nots and buttercups, and alive with the constant hum of bees and the chatter of birdsong.

Here Laurel would sometimes escape in her lunch break, to sit on a wooden seat, munching an apple and letting the contentment of this serene spot seep slowly into her soul, applying a balm it was increasingly difficult for her to find these days. And here, one day, Robert found her.

'It gets more of a pull, climbing that hill, as one gets older,' he said, easing himself on to the seat beside her. She saw that he was indeed breathing very hard, almost panting, and beads of perspiration dampened his forehead. 'There's no way of escaping the heat this year either!'

'It *is* hot,' Laurel agreed carefully. She was torn by a need to ask him straight out if that was all that was bothering him, but bit her lip, remembering Ana's plea that she should say nothing.

'But there's a breeze here, and it's peaceful,' Robert went on, and there was a note of thankfulness in his voice, a tranquillity about him that was altogether new, and not only in these last few weeks. Robert had always been a restless, forceful, energetic man, not noted for his calmness.

'I always think this is more like God's garden than anything else one can imagine,' he went on. 'I think I'd rather like to be buried here.'

Laurel shot him a sharp glance.

'I'll bear it in mind, but we aren't thinking of sticking you in a box yet awhile!' she told him, her voice hoarse with affection.

He laughed—another sound which had been absent from his repertoire of late, and put an arm round her shoulder.

'Little Laurel—my little girl,' he said, and she buried her face in the smooth tweed of his summer-weight jacket, and slid her arm round his waist. 'Is it going well for you? Is he treating you fairly, that man I sold out to?'

A few weeks earlier she might have been tempted to blurt out the trials and tribulations of her relationship with Trent, without asking herself if Robert was up to taking on her problems.

Now she only said, 'Yes. He's exacting to work for, but fair.' Which was the truth, as far as it went. She was reluctant to burden Robert with her troubles, since she could not rid herself of the notion that he had greater ones of his own. If it would ease his mind to know that she was happy, both in her personal and working life, then that was the part she would play.

Unable to resist putting the question, in spite of Ana's request, she lifted her head and looked into his eyes.

'Dad? Is everything all right? Are you...are you well?'

'Never better,' he said firmly. 'I told you, it's just the heat that's getting to me.' Smiling, he patted her head. 'Off with you now, back to work. I'm sure your lunch hour must be nearly over, and I don't want to get you into trouble with the boss.'

Laurel watched him set off slowly down the path to the churchyard gate. She was full of vague, unspecified forebodings, sure that no matter what he had told her, all was not well. But what could she do, if he insisted so emphatically that it was? He was a mature adult man who would not stand for any interference in what he considered to be his own business.

Tears of frustration and worry were only just being held at bay as Laurel hurried back to the Caterplus building, and, to make matters worse, she almost bumped into Trent in the corridor.

'I was looking for you,' he said briskly. 'Can you let me have those breakdown figures on the Southern Inns contract some time this afternoon? Preferably before three o'clock.'

Laurel was too anxious and uptight to hide her impatience at this seemingly impossible demand.

'It's a bit short notice,' she said. 'If you'd told me this morning, I could have started work on them earlier.'

'Had I known this morning, I could have told you,' he said coldly. 'Not that I'm obliged to give you an explanation for everything I ask you to do, but I was tied up with Southern Inn's directors until lunchtime, hence the need for the figures before I see them again tomorrow. You have to get used to thinking on your feet when you work for Castleford.'

'And standing on your head too, no doubt,' she flashed back, with a touch of her old animosity. 'Aren't Castleford's employees allowed to be human, to have problems and commitments other than what happens at work?'

Her dark eyes were swimming with unshed tears, and she knew that it was both wrong and silly to attempt to take out on Trent her anxiety about her father. That was not the way a mature and competent businesswoman was supposed to behave, and would only ensure that his respect for her capabilities would fly out of the window along with his desire for her as a woman.

Surprisingly, instead of giving her a dressing down, he laid a cool hand on her arm and said perceptively, 'This isn't about Southern Inns' contract, is it Laurel? There's something else.'

It was the closest thing to a personal conversation they'd had in weeks—come to think of it, the first time in ages he'd used her Christian name. The entirely unexpected sympathy caused Laurel's strained emotions to break their leash.

'It's my father!' she burst out, unable to keep it in any longer. She had to confide in someone, and Trent seemed to be the only one whose strength and detachment rarely failed. 'I'm convinced he's not well, but he keeps on insisting to Ana and myself that he is, and I don't know what to do!'

He looked down at her, disbelief etched across his face, and finally he shook his head slightly.

'Sometimes, Laurel, you can't see beyond the end of that not very large nose of yours,' he said exasperatedly, and she returned his gaze with a puzzled stare.

'What do you mean?'

'I mean I would have thought it blindingly obvious that your father's retirement was a necessity, not a choice, and that health was the reason for it. I don't know why you couldn't see that on the day we met, except that you were too wrapped up in how the take-over of the company was going to affect you. But I would have thought you'd have worked it out for yourself by now.'

There was a faint, dismissive scorn in his voice, and Laurel flinched. But she forced herself to concentrate on the all-important issue of her father's health, and tried not to be too hurt by Trent's low opinion of her.

'Did he tell you anything about his reasons when you negotiated the take-over?'

'No, he did not, nor was it my business to ask,' Trent said sharply. 'I'm merely using my common sense and powers of observation. But surely your stepmother would have noticed anything amiss.'

'She was worried about him while they were on holiday,' Laurel answered slowly, thoughtfully. 'But now...it's odd...I think she's trying to pretend everything is back to normal again.'

'Perhaps that's her way of dealing with whatever it is,' he suggested.

Laurel almost stamped her foot in distraction.

'But that's crazy! If there's something wrong, it needs to be dealt with!' she cried. 'Trent, I——'

From his office, she heard the telephone shrill out, and then Gloria bustled out.

'Sorry to interrupt,' she excused herself, 'but I've finally managed to get hold of that...party you wanted to speak to, and she's in rather a hurry.'

'Right,' Trent said promptly. He looked down at Laurel with a little frown. 'Look, Laurel, I have to take this call.'

Whatever it was, it appeared to be more important than her problems, Laurel thought miserably as she hurried back to her office. Well, after all, why should he concern himself with her?

But what he had said had only confirmed her own gloomy suspicions, and she admitted that he was right. She had been stupid and blinkered not to have guessed the truth from the outset. Robert was not well, despite his insistent denials.

But she still did not know what, if anything, she could do about it, and it was ironic that she felt the need to turn to Trent for advice. When she finally took along the breakdown figures, after having worked like a slave all afternoon and finishing them by three-thirty, only half an hour later than he had asked for them, she was determined to talk to him further. He might be hard and ruthless in some ways, but what he said was usually clearly thought out and to the point.

However, the door to the connecting office was firmly closed, and Gloria took the papers from her.

'I'll see he gets them,' she said. 'Right now he's asked not to be disturbed.'

'Oh.' Laurel bit her full lower lip disappointedly. 'I was hoping for a word. Do you think...'

Gloria's shake of the head was emphatic.

'Oh, my dear, I wouldn't recommend going in there, for your own safety!' she said. 'That phone call he had earlier—I've never seen him look like that before. Dazed—you know, as if he wasn't sure which way to turn. Usually he's so dynamic and certain. I reckon he still feels more for her than he lets on.'

'Her?' Laurel queried ominously, knowing by now what she was going to hear, and hating it.

'Yes, *her*. Cara Peretta, of course. Don't you read the newspapers, Laurel?' Gloria pushed a copy of a local paper across her desk. 'My sister is an opera fan, she pointed this out to me. Cara Peretta will be here next week, to sing at Glyndebourne. And they were on the phone for simply ages this afternoon. Do you know, it wouldn't surprise me one little bit if there were a reconciliation in prospect! What do *you* think?'

CHAPTER NINE

LAUREL had never been a devotee of the opera, so although she had driven many times past the gracious old mansion in the jewel setting of its parkland, surrounded by the green folds of the Downs, she had never seen the curtain rise in the intimate, red-plush auditorium, or picnicked in evening dress from a hamper of smoked salmon, strawberries and champagne on the lawns outside.

But Trent was going to do so, she knew, for Gloria had informed her that he had brought his evening suit in to the office to avoid having to go back to Palmeira Square to change. She hadn't expected to see him attired in it, but while she was conferring with Gloria about agenda items for a meeting he emerged from his inner office looking sleek and elegant, the smooth black of the suit enhancing the brushed gold of his hair.

Laurel's heart constricted, and it was in that moment that she finally admitted the truth she had long refused to face. I'm in love with him, she thought, of course I am. Not just attracted, not simply bowled over by the intense physical reactions he induced in her, although that was unchanged, but in love. The heady, hopeless yearning, the sick excitement whenever she saw him, the disappointment when she did not—what else could it mean?

How she recognised this state so surely, never having been in love before, was a mystery to her. It had to be a purely instinctive knowledge, something in the blood that we all know when inevitably we come slap up against it. Something we can't deny, which gives us a perverse pleasure even when it causes us most pain.

She took refuge in jocularity.

'My, my, aren't we smart?' she said, mock-admiringly. 'Have you got your hamper of goodies ready for the interval?'

'It's being delivered,' he said coolly, with a little condescending smile. 'Instead of being facetious, you should get your best bib and tucker out and come to a performance. A little culture wouldn't do you any harm, and you might even learn something.'

'My crinoline's at the dry-cleaners,' she retorted spiritedly.

'Of course, I forgot, you draw the line at Gilbert and Sullivan, don't you?' Trent flung back over his shoulder as he retreated into his office, from where she heard him singing, softly and mockingly,

'The flowers that bloom in the spring, tra-la,
Have nothing to do with the case.
I've got to take under my wing, tra-la,
A most unattractive old thing, tra-la,
With a caricature of a face!'

Gloria looked dumbfoundedly from the half-open door to Laurel's face, and back again.

'What on earth was all that about?' she whispered, mystified.

'Best not to ask,' Laurel said wryly.

Trent had been in a strange mood all week, half buoyant, half sombre, and it could not be coincidence that Cara Peretta was around. Laurel had seen photographs of her in the local paper, and the star's appearance had surprised her. She had expected Cara to be dark and dramatic, a statuesque Italianate beauty, but she was slim and fair, almost wraithlike, with silvery blonde hair and calm, widely spaced eyes. There was a wistful, haunting loveliness about her that wrung the heart, and Laurel had to remind herself that this woman could no way be as fragile as she looked.

She had survived and triumphed in a hard, competitive world that demanded stamina along with artistic merit, and she had turned her back on the man who loved her, for the sake of that world. She had to be candyfloss around a core of steel.

Trent was hard too, in his own way, but Laurel sensed the difference. With him, the shell was on the outside. He was capable of being hurt, and Cara, so it seemed, was the only one whose arrows could pierce the shell.

During the last few days he had functioned with his usual dedicated tenacity, missing no detail, on top of everything, and woe betide anyone who failed to keep up the pace. Yet it seemed to Laurel that beneath the efficient surface he was engaged in a titanic struggle with his emotions.

She herself had guessed, and later learned to her cost, that Trent's feelings for his wife had never really died, only gone underground. She had seen how easily a memory, a thought, a snatched fragment of song could bring them bursting back to vibrant, painful life.

Yet Trent was no one's fool. He knew how it felt to take a back seat to Cara's career. 'I couldn't sit around waiting for any woman's favours,' he had said emphatically. Would that have changed, or had he come regretfully to the conclusion, after seeing Cara again, that whatever the cost to himself, he had to have her back in his life?

After all, Laurel thought wretchedly, she knew how he felt. If he wanted her, now, she would go to him. She wouldn't be as high-minded and fastidious as she had been in Normandy. She had learned what it was to love.

Just then, he stuck his head round the door and called out, 'Can you come in here a minute, please, Laurel?'

A minute? A month, a lifetime, my love, she thought, and, putting on as calm a face as she could muster, she answered his summons.

'Close the door,' he said, and she obeyed, heart pounding wildly. But he only asked quietly, 'How are things at home now, Laurel?'

His concern touched her, even though she knew it was no more than the almost avuncular interest of an employer for a colleague, and she shook her head.

'Quiet enough, but nothing has changed. My father contends that there's nothing wrong with him other than a dislike of the hot weather. Ana goes along with that, and I have the feeling she knows it's not true.' She sighed. 'Sometimes I tell myself that maybe I'm imagining things, and there really is nothing to worry about.'

She looked at him hopefully from beneath lowered dark lashes. 'But *you* don't believe that, do you?'

His face was gravely impassive.

'I don't know him as well as you do, obviously. And I have been known to be wrong.'

'No? Really?' There was just a flash of the old impish Laurel in her response, but in her heart she was wondering if he were admitting his own error in believing he was through with Cara.

He smiled wryly, and a brief moment of dark humour drew them together before he said, 'Only occasionally, of course. I won't confess to more than that.' Becoming brisk and professional again, he said, 'What I wanted to tell you, Laurel, was this. I've invited a few key members of staff along to my flat for drinks, Sunday lunchtime, and I'd like you to be there. Twelve-thirty all right for you? I shall have a small announcement to make.'

A small announcement? Dread began to build up in Laurel's heart, but she struggled hard to keep calm, not to let ideas run away with her. Why should Trent gather together members of Caterplus personnel to announce that he was getting together again with his ex-wife—if, indeed, that were the case? On the other hand, why the socialising element? The meetings-room here would have done for official business.

'Yes, I...think I can make it,' she agreed, knowing that this was not really an invitation but a command. And hating herself, but unable to prevent the question from bursting out, she added faintly, 'Will...will your ex-wife be there?'

'Cara?' He looked surprised, and Laurel's keenly attuned ears thought she detected a note of fond amusement. 'I shouldn't think so. I could invite her, if the thought of hobnobbing with the famous appeals to you, but I doubt if she'll come. Cara hates parties of any kind. Someone might smoke, you see, and it would be bad for her voice. What's more, business, and business people, bore her.'

She sounds like a crashing bore herself, Laurel thought, wondering how a man of Trent's intelligence could let such a woman get a hold on him.

'Oh, we couldn't allow that! I should hate to bore anyone,' she said cattily.

Trent smiled, a world-weary, regretful smile, and as his eyes held hers she felt the world slow down, her pulse, her breathing, her very heartbeat suspend itself for what seemed an eternity crammed into an instant. He lifted his hand and lightly brushed her shining dark hair, his fingers lingering a moment against her cheek.

I wish it could have happened for us too, she thought he seemed to be saying. We were almost there, but just not quite close enough, and now the chance has gone, and won't come again.

'I don't think there'll ever be any danger of that,' he said softly, opening the door, and without stopping to speak to Gloria, or wondering what she might think, Laurel stumbled blindly out.

The sun was sparkling the bluest of seas as Laurel drove along the front at Brighton and turned into Palmeira Square. The elegant Georgian buildings set around the green oasis of the central gardens were brilliant white and mellow cream, the brightness of the day lending them an ambience that was almost Mediterranean, and it was hot enough to make one believe one was in Cannes rather than in Sussex.

Laurel wore a sleeveless white cotton dress, her narrow waist cinched by a wide black belt, and before getting out of the car she slipped off the comfortable flat shoes she had driven in and put on black patent sandals with three-inch heels to add height to her stature. She had pinned up her hair too, and the total effect was of extreme sophistication.

She hoped all this morale-boosting would carry her through. Having no idea why Trent had summoned them to his flat, she was apprehensive about whatever he had to say; moreover, simply being in a room with him was enough to unnerve her now.

The living-room of the apartment was vast, with windows open to a balcony with views of the sea. A long table was spread with buffet food, and Laurel saw that she was the last person to arrive—everyone already had plates and glasses filled. Alan was there, and Robin and Ken, Janet and Gloria, several more of the Caterplus hierarchy. They all seemed relaxed and at ease, chatting among themselves; only she, it appeared, was nervous and unsure.

'You're late,' Trent reprimanded her, filling her glass with sparkling Lambrusco. 'In the circumstances, that's not encouraging, but since it's unusual for you, I'll overlook it.'

The reason for her lateness was Clive, who had arrived just before she was about to set off, and kept her talking in the hall. Johnny was pressing him about the partnership, and he simply had to have a serious discussion with her.

'OK, but not now, Clive,' she had begged, looking at her watch, knowing how Trent felt about unpunctuality. 'I can't see what the problem is—the partnership sounds like a good deal to me. However, if you want to talk, fine, but now just isn't convenient.'

'*Him* again, is it?' he had demanded sulkily, and when battle flared in Laurel's eyes, he backed off. 'All right— I said I wouldn't mention him, I'm sorry!'

'It's a business occasion,' she had told him firmly. Now, looking up into Trent's face, she said, 'What circumstances? I don't understand.'

'You will,' he said mysteriously, and moving into the middle of the circle, he raised a hand and said, 'Can I have a bit of hush, please, everyone?'

The chatter died down, and everyone looked at him expectantly. Trent smiled.

'I hope you're all enjoying the buffet,' he said. 'You'll be aware that it's from the Caterplus gourmet range, and I didn't do that simply so that I could capitalise on Robin's usefulness...' here a ripple of laughter ran around the room '...but because I believe, in fact, I *know* it's the best.'

They were all listening intently now, and Laurel's teeth bit into her lower lip so hard that she tasted blood. Everyone knew that something significant was coming, and in the sudden quiet, the hum of the traffic along the parade, and the sigh of waves crunching the beach were clearly audible.

'Everyone who works at Caterplus will find they have a bonus in their next wage or salary packet,' Trent went on. 'That's my way of saying thank you, not only for your hard work, but for giving me the chance to merit your loyalty. All I ask of you is more of the same, and the gloomy Jeremiahs who knock the British workforce will have me to answer to. The toast is—the good ship Caterplus, and all who sail in her!'

He raised his glass, smiling round at the assembled company, and from the rear, Robin's voice said, 'And the captain!'

When the laughter had died down, Trent continued more seriously.

'That brings me nicely to the subject I wanted to broach.

'I've been with you for almost six months now, and expansion plans, as you all know, are well under way. It's time for me to move on and inaugurate other projects in Europe.'

Laurel stood silent, her hand gripping the stem of her glass, while inside her something died. So that was it! He was going away, as she had always known one day he would. Going away and taking with him the heart she had given him, neither knowing nor caring, nor wanting it. She could not have spoken or moved at that moment. It took all her resolve simply to remain standing there, doing her damnedest to appear unconcerned.

'I shall naturally be keeping a watching brief on Caterplus,' he told them. 'And sooner or later, a permanent managing director will be appointed, who may or may not be the person I have chosen to act in that capacity in the meantime.'

The silence was once again absolute.

'The acting appointment has been approved by Castleford's board, but no one gets on in this outfit other than by merit, so it will be up to that person to prove her worth.'

Laurel could not breathe as his eyes met hers over the heads of the assembled gathering, because he had deliberately given it away. *Her* worth, he had said, and that could only mean…could only mean… She clutched the back of a chair as the world spun dizzily around her.

'Yes, of course, it's Laurel,' Trent said with a smile. 'She's young—but I believe she's capable, and I know she will have your full support.'

Everyone was crowding around Laurel, kissing her and slapping her on the back, congratulating her and filling her glass, all talking at once. She was too dumbfounded to do anything but smile her thanks. Her eyes desperately sought Trent, but he had deliberately withdrawn himself, as if to say he was no longer really a part of all this, his job was done, and now it was over to her.

It was a while before she could escape the attention concentrated on her, but after the party had settled down again, and everyone was talking and drinking, she looked around for Trent and found him over the far side of the room. He was leaning composedly against a bookshelf and listening to music that was playing softly on the deck of the stereo unit.

Laurel knew the singer's identity at once. Over the last week, a painful but irresistible curiosity had impelled her to buy several recordings by Cara Peretta, and now she heard again the brilliant soprano voice, soaring over its range with the apparent effortlessness born of years of unremitting dedication, and the depths of emotion that no teacher could ever impart, if it were not there.

'Mozart,' he said. 'The duet between the Don and Zerlina from *Don Giovanni*. She'll be singing Zerlina at the Mozart Festival in Salzburg in August. Before that, *Traviata* at La Scala in Milan.'

Now she understood. Cara would be performing all over Europe this summer, and there would be many occasions when his travels and hers would coincide. He'd make sure there were. In the beautiful, romantic Austrian city of Salzburg with its baroque buildings and sublime mountain setting, in pulsating Milan, in Italy, with its memories of their student days and their early married years...they would be together, renewing their relationship, his fascination with her flaring up again.

It did not really matter if he and Cara became reconciled or not, in one sense, for the tragedy was not their possible remarriage, but his continued involvement with her on an emotional level. Bound by that, he could never be wholly free or wholly happy with any other woman. Perhaps it was best that he went away, Laurel thought. If he ever offered her the dregs of himself, she might just be desperate enough to accept, and that could be disastrous.

'I wanted to thank you for having faith in me,' she said tremulously.

'Don't thank me. It isn't a gift—you earned it,' he told her. 'Furthermore, it isn't without strings.'

His tawny brows narrowed as he concentrated his gaze on her.

'I recommended the appointment before I knew you had problems at home,' he said. 'I only hope it won't prove too much for you.'

Her chin went up.

'I give my word that, when I'm at work, my attention will be a hundred and ten per cent on what I'm doing. It won't suffer,' she said proudly.

'That wasn't what I meant,' he said, his eyes suddenly cold and hard. 'But I suppose you've got what you wanted most in the world now, Laurel. I hope it makes you happy.'

She did not—could not—contradict him. Impossible to tell him that ambition no longer ruled her life as she had once blithely assumed it always would. Impossible to admit that she had discovered the full glory and sadness of her own womanhood, her own humanity. And now she had what she once fought him for, wasn't it ironic that *he* himself had become what she wanted most—and could not have?

Laurel was subdued and quiet when she met Clive in the bar of the White Hart one evening soon after, and she imparted her tremendous news without great emotion.

'I'm very, very proud of you,' Robert had said quietly when she told him. 'Whether it's the right road for such a young and pretty woman, I'm still not convinced, but if Trent Castleford is prepared to give you a chance, and it's what you want, I won't knock it. Eh, Ana?'

'She is a very clever girl,' Ana agreed with awe and pride. 'But I should like to be a stepgrandmama one day. This does not help my case.'

They had laughed and opened a bottle of champagne, and their happiness for her had eased a little of the pain in Laurel's heart. She did not expect Clive to be in approval of her meteoric promotion. He had made no secret of how he saw a woman's role—but she was surprised and more than a little annoyed when he hit the roof.

'Good lord, Laurel, that's ridiculous!' he protested, so loudly that several heads turned in their direction. 'What can that man Castleford be thinking of, putting a slip of a girl in charge of a company!'

'It's not just any company, it's Caterplus, and I've grown up with it!' she reminded him hotly. 'And I am *not* a slip of a girl, but a grown woman of twenty-one! What's the difference between that and your going into partnership with Johnny Willis?'

'All the difference in the world. How can you possibly do such a demanding job when you're married?'

'The question is purely hypothetical. Who am I likely to marry?'

The question was asked with a wealth of self-mockery, not seriously expecting an answer, and her jaw dropped open with amazement when he said, totally out of the blue, 'Why, me, of course. Who else?'

Taking advantage of her stunned silence, he pressed on, 'Isn't it the obvious answer, for both of us? You may not think this a romantic proposal, but we've known each other most of our lives, and we get on well, most of the time. I've been very good lately, because I thought that was the way you wanted me to play it, but you know I fancy you.'

'Stop it, Clive!' Laurel said sharply. 'This has to be a macabre joke! I don't love you, and nothing you've said makes me think you love me. I can't think why you would want to marry me. Certainly I can't marry *you*. Not now, not ever!'

A sullen look crept into his eyes, like that of a schoolboy denied a treat.

'And there, I suppose, is the reason why not!' he hissed at her, jerking his head towards the door. Laurel followed the direction of his stare with horrified fascination, and there was Trent, with a woman on his arm. A woman of blonde, ethereal slenderness, with a fragile, fine-boned face that made heads turn in recognition as she passed, awarding everyone a gracious little smile, as if they were all her audience.

Laurel was transfixed. She forgot Clive and his ridiculous proposal, forgot that she was a young, successful executive with a brilliant future. All she could see, all she could think about, was the man she loved, sitting across the room with the woman *he* loved. She had never known that there could be such pain; she dared not take a normal breath for fear something vital inside her would tear and injure her.

'Wake up, Laurel, and stop being a fool,' Clive snapped with angry petulance. 'You're wasting your time! Come and see me when you come to your senses— I've better things to do than waste mine!'

Laurel hardly registered his abrupt, clumsy exit, almost knocking over several chairs as he slammed out. Under any other circumstances, it would have been embarrassing to be left alone in a public bar, but she was too absorbed by her own agony to have room to spare for such trivial emotions.

Only when she caught Trent's eyes on her and realised he had witnessed the undignified little scene, a rush of discomfiture overcame her, and she rose swiftly to leave. She saw Trent excuse himself to the woman at his side, saw Cara's forehead pucker in annoyance, and quickened her pace.

She had made the doorway when he caught her, and even now, the touch of his hand on her arm made her quiver.

'Laurel, are you all right?'

'Let me go, Trent. I'm fine. Everything's fine,' she lied wildly.

'Oh, yes? Come off it, Laurel, I know you better than that. Was that lout bothering you again?'

She looked up defiantly into his face. Who did he think he was? Since he did not care for her, why should he think he could interfere in her life like some concerned uncle figure? While that woman sat there tapping her fingers on the table with possessive impatience!

'That "lout", as you mistakenly call him, has just asked me to marry him!' she declared.

A shadow flickered across his face.

'I assume you turned him down?'

'Then don't assume!' snapped Laurel. 'Maybe I just need more time to think about it. Maybe it's not such a bad idea after all—and who are you to sling bricks? Or is it only Castleford's *male* executives who are allowed to have a private life in tandem with their jobs?'

He let go of her arm with a sudden gesture of resigned disgust.

'Your private life is your own business, as you so aptly point out. Go right ahead and learn from your own mistakes.'

'It looks as if you didn't!' Laurel flung at him, and turning, fled headlong into the street.

Laurel had never thought it would be easy, sitting in the seat which Robert had occupied for so many years, and which Trent had so ably taken over. She had been fully prepared for even harder, longer hours of work than she had hitherto known, and she realised that she could function only as the head of an efficient and loyal team, who backed her every inch of the way.

What no one could have prepared her for was the essential loneliness at the top, the knowledge that, when it came to the crunch, the final decisions were hers, and, having made them, she would have the agonised hours of wondering if she had acted rightly or wrongly. She could only wait and hope that would lessen as time passed and her confidence in her judgement grew.

Meanwhile, she was almost glad that work demanded all her waking hours and all her energy, leaving her no time to mope or brood on her inner misery.

She had not realised that when she had run away from Trent that night at the White Hart she would not be seeing him again. During the days since he had announced her promotion, he had gradually initiated her into the ways of Castleford's higher management echelons, passing on useful snippets of information it would have taken her months to discover for herself, showing her the way things worked at the heart of the vast organisation. Preparing her for her role. He had been impersonal and professional, behaving towards her with a cool formality, and, while she found that painful, at least he had been *there*.

And suddenly he was gone, without warning. His things were cleared from his desk, his appointments diary had a line drawn across it, and even Gloria swore she'd had no idea, the night before, that he wouldn't be there in the morning.

'Maybe it was a sudden decision, or maybe he'd planned to go like that, without any fuss,' she said. 'An enigma to the last. But my sister tells me Cara Peretta has sung her last performance at Glyndebourne and is due to sing at La Scala next week.'

Enough said, Laurel thought miserably, plunging herself so deeply into the task at hand that for the next two weeks she staggered home at night too exhausted to do more than eat dinner and fall into bed by nine-thirty.

'This is not right!' Ana said worriedly, one night in early July. 'Robert, will you put sense into this daughter of yours! She cannot go on like this.'

Robert smiled gently.

'Laurel must go her own way, my dear, as we all must,' he said. 'She's a woman now, and no longer our little girl. But Ana's right.' He looked at Laurel with just a hint of his old stern authority. 'Ease off a bit. The company doesn't need your blood. Leave a bit of something for the rest of your life.'

He patted her arm fondly as he got up.

'I'm just going to spend an hour or so in the study,' he said. 'Remember what I just told you.'

The last thing Laurel wanted was for him to be worried on her account.

'It's only until I get on top of the job,' she promised, with a smile. 'I'll remember. Not that I'll have to—I'm sure you'll remind me again.'

She had not an inkling of how those words would return to haunt her.

She made herself sit and watch a film on the video with Ana, and looked lonely, and finally went up to bed at ten-thirty. For some reason, tired as she was, she could not settle. She kept seeing Trent's face before her eyes, as he had looked at her across the restaurant table in Honfleur, full of a fierce, tender need she had failed to satisfy. Would it have made any difference if she had? Could her love have kept him from his obsession with Cara? She would never know. At last, after tossing restlessly for a long time, Laurel dropped into a heavy, exhaustion-drugged sleep.

She was woken by the most terrible scream she had ever heard, like something out of a nightmare, so that at first sitting bolt upright, trembling, she thought that must have been what it was. Composing herself for sleep again, telling herself she had only been dreaming, she heard it again, this time louder, clearer, curdling the blood in her veins. A scream of terror and desperation, reverberating through the darkness until the whole house echoed with it.

The voice was Ana's.

'No!' she shrieked mindlessly. 'No, no, no, no!'

Laurel was out of bed in the split fraction of a second between the screams. Barefoot and in only her nightdress, she sped downstairs on wings of pure reaction, running along the corridor towards Robert's study, from where the screams were emanating, not even feeling the pain as her shin caught the sharp edge of the hall table as she cornered unevenly.

The light from Robert's desk-top anglepoise lamp cut a swathe across the room and into the corridor, and

Laurel gasped, horror seizing her as she stopped abruptly in the doorway.

Ana was crouched on the floor, head on her bent knees, arms covering her head in a foetal position. Her screams had subsided to an unearthly keening that was at the same time pathetic and chilling, a sound that was barely human.

Robert sat in the large wing chair behind his desk, his hands clenched over the arms, his head fallen back and his eyes wide open, staring.

He was quite dead.

CHAPTER TEN

LOOKING back on that night, in time still to come, Laurel often wondered where she found the strength to deal with it. Woken abruptly from sleep to a reality far worse than any nightmare, for a moment she had stood fixed to the ground in deep shock, and it would have taken very little to push her over the brink into a reaction of helpless distress.

Instead, after that moment of paralysis, a blessed, ice-cold numbness set in, allowing her to function efficiently. She felt Robert's pulse briefly, although she scarcely needed confirmation that he was dead, picked up the phone and quietly rang their family doctor. Then she put her arms around the shaking, hysterical Ana and somehow half persuaded, half carried her out of the study and into the lounge, where she sat holding her stepmother in her arms until the doctor arrived. She could not leave her long enough to make a cup of tea or even pour a brandy, for Ana clung on to her, trembling and sobbing brokenly, her grief frightening in its animal intensity.

'You did the right thing,' the doctor told her. 'I shall have to sedate her—she can't cope with this all at once. But I think a brandy would be in order for you. And is there anyone you'd like to call who would stay with you?'

Oh, yes, and how she longed to have Trent's steady arms round her, his calm assurance a barrier between herself and the grief she was barely holding at bay!

'I'll be all right on my own,' she insisted, thinking that she could not possibly face Clive until the morning. She shook her head, racked by guilt. 'I should have nagged my father harder into coming to see you. Perhaps if I had, he'd still be alive now.'

'No.' The doctor was gently but firmly reassuring. 'There was nothing you could have done. I recommended him to a heart specialist before Christmas, and he told Robert there was no treatment that could save him. He knew he had only a short time left, but he was adamant no one must know—not even your stepmother. He said he wanted to live his remaining days without everyone treating him as a semi-invalid.'

He had known. All the time he was pretending to be suffering only from the heat, and before that, when he had taken Ana to the Caribbean. When he'd sold Caterplus, he had already been under a death sentence, and all she, Laurel, had done was harangue him about cheating her out of what she felt was hers!

She sat through that bleak night after the doctor had left and the undertakers had been, asking herself over and over again why she had been so blind, so selfish. Trent had understood immediately why Robert was selling, even if he had not realised the full extent of his illness. Why had it taken *her* so long?

Because I was nothing more than a silly, immature, self-centred girl, she thought wretchedly, for all I believed I was so bright and efficient and capable of anything!

She had trodden a long, hard road of growing up this year, and only tonight, in her loneliness, she finally took stock of the price she had paid for her new and bitter maturity.

The days that followed brought her little respite. Ana, once the sedative wore off, was wild with grief, refusing to eat or to attend to simple matters such as brushing her hair or dressing herself. She sat huddled in her dressing-gown in the bedroom she and Robert had shared, weeping continuously. She would allow no one but Laurel near her, and on the day after Robert's death Laurel phoned the office and told Alan they would have to manage without her, at least until after the funeral.

'Don't worry about it,' he said promptly. 'Take as long as you need—we'll manage. Everyone here is so stunned, but it must be far worse for you and Ana. If there's anything at all we can do, you need only ask.'

Touched, she rang off and returned to sit with her stricken stepmother, holding her hand and talking to her softly, trying vainly to offer comfort where there was none to be found. Her own grief she held down fiercely, refusing to let it spill over, for how could she ever cope if she gave way to her emotions?

'The funeral is tomorrow,' Clive said testily, pacing the floor of the lounge. 'Ana's going to have to pull herself together before then!'

'Pull herself together!' Laurel stared at him disbelievingly. 'She's just lost the man she loved!'

'I know, but she can't carry on like this. We're all shocked, we're all upset, but life has to go on,' he shrugged. 'For me, this couldn't have come at a worse time. Johnny's really pressuring me over this partnership deal, and I can't stall him much longer.'

Laurel pushed a weary hand through the thick, dark locks she'd had no time to wash.

'Then go ahead. I can't think what's preventing you,' she said tiredly.

'Sometimes you really are dense, Laurel!' Clive exclaimed. 'Money's preventing me, that's what! On account of how I don't have any!'

'You mean what your father left you isn't enough?' Laurel could hear Ana's sobs increasing in volume, and knew she must go to her, but Clive suddenly took her by the shoulders and shook her like a rag doll.

'You little idiot—there isn't any! I spent it all years ago!' he cried. 'Yes, I know it was stupid of me, yes, I know I shouldn't have, and yes, I regret it now, because this deal with Johnny is a good one, and I really want to do it! Damn it, Laurel, you've got to help me! You're the only one who can!'

Between the hysterically crying woman upstairs, and the distraught young man shouting at her and bruising her skin with his harsh grip, Laurel felt her overstretched resources of strength and endurance come dangerously close to snapping.

So that was the reason for Clive's crazy proposal of marriage! She had known he wasn't in love with her, but could not have guessed he was after the money he knew very well she stood to inherit on marriage, the money from the sale of Caterplus!

Taking a deep, calming breath, she detached herself from his grasp and stepped back.

'I can't touch the money Father left me until I'm twenty-five, you know that,' she said. 'The rest of his estate is willed first to Ana, and I won't have her worried by your financial problems. Damn it, Clive, she couldn't even take it in right now!'

For a moment she thought he was too overwrought to heed what she said. Then his shoulders sagged dejectedly, his face fell, and she knew a brief pity. He wasn't really bad, just weak, and the garden centre deal might be his last chance of redemption.

'After the funeral, we'll talk,' she promised more gently. 'I'll help if I can, see if there are ways of raising a loan. For now, please, just go away and let me get on with what has to be done.'

Towards evening, Ana fell into an exhausted sleep, and the house was blessedly quiet. Laurel, dropping with fatigue but hardly daring to catch a brief nap in case she was needed again, took and pressed Ana's black suit and her own plain black dress for the funeral, and checked that the house was in readiness for the guests who would be coming back after the service and burial.

Bone-weary, full of an aching sadness but unable to allow herself the luxury of tears for fear she might give way completely and fail to cope, she went into the kitchen and made herself a cup of coffee. Sitting at the breakfast bar sipping the scalding liquid without really tasting it, she was startled by the ring of the front doorbell, echoing loudly through the silent house.

Now what? she thought wretchedly, dragging herself down the corridor, anxious only to get rid of whoever it was, and be left alone.

She opened the door unthinkingly, and there he stood in the doorway. Tall and strong and sure, not smiling but with eyes that spoke worlds of compassion and reassurance, a flight bag in one hand, his jacket slung over his other arm. The warmth of his body, the breadth of his shoulders, the wonderful masculine scent and aura of him, all there, only an arm's length away. A miracle!

'Trent!' she gasped faintly. 'Oh, Trent!'

And then he had only time to drop both bag and jacket on the floor before her world went black, and he caught her in his arms.

*   *   *

The evening sun was slanting across the old orchard as Trent drew the car to a halt outside the cottage, and the countryside was mellow and peaceful in its golden light. The grass had been mown short, the stream gurgled pleasantly and as Trent unlocked the front door, Laurel caught the scent of fresh paint and plaster. There were rugs on the floor, chintz curtains at the windows, and traditional, comfortable furniture that blended perfectly with the serene 'country' look. Logs were already piled in the vast fireplace, and a tabby cat followed them in, tail in the air, as if it owned the place.

'I call her Babette,' Trent said. 'She doesn't appear to have an owner, so I feed her when I'm here, and I suspect she freelances the rest of the time.'

He set the bag of groceries they had bought in the village shop on the table of the newly refitted kitchen—a long baguette, pâté, cheese, tomatoes, eggs and a bottle of the strong local cider.

'Make yourself at home,' he invited.

'Oh, no—I want to help,' Laurel said awkwardly.

'That's exactly what I meant. I haven't brought you here in order to wait on you,' he said cheerfully. 'Grate some cheese and beat the eggs in a bowl ready for the omelettes. The kitchen is so small you'll soon find everything.'

They had laid Robert Ashby to rest in the churchyard among the wild flowers only the day before, and it was a measure of the respect and affection he had enjoyed locally that the church had been virtually full for the service.

Clive had turned up, quiet and restrained in his dark suit, to offer Ana his arm as she stood with stoic, marvellous dignity, dry-eyed and fully in command of herself.

Laurel, a little shaky but composed, was endlessly grateful for the solidity and firmness of Trent at her side.

She remembered little of the first few hours after his miraculous arrival on her doorstep. She had fainted—the first time ever in her life—and he must have carried her indoors, and then, when she came round, she had wept long and helplessly in his arms, sobbing out guilt, regret and grief, until it was all a blur, and she had fallen into a deep, profound sleep.

When she woke it was to find herself in bed, with Ana sitting beside her, as she had done whenever Laurel was ill when she was younger. Ana, smiling gravely and perfectly calm, with a bowl of soup at the ready for Laurel to drink.

'Ana...you're all right?' she managed to mumble.

'Yes, *pobrecita*, as you see,' her stepmother replied. 'I am sorry I scared you, but the Latin way of dealing with grief is not stiff upper lip, like the Anglo-Saxon,' she explained quietly. 'Now I suffer—but I will survive, because I let it all out. But I made you bottle up your feelings, and that was not good. You have had to deal with everything, my poor child.'

Laurel smiled weakly.

'We'll help one another now,' she said, and glancing over Ana's shoulder, saw Trent appear in the doorway. 'I didn't dream it, then—it really *is* you,' she said.

'It really is me. Drink your soup,' he commanded, and when she obeyed without demur he nodded his satisfaction and left them, saying, 'I'll go and make coffee.'

After Laurel had finished the soup, Ana took the tray and set it on the bedside table, then resumed her place on the bed.

'I have been having such a good talk with Señor Castleford—*Trent*,' she corrected herself warmly. 'He has been very helpful, and with his assistance, I have come to a decision. You see, *querida*, I don't think I could bear to stay in this house after the funeral. Too many memories. I need to get away for a while, and I thought how good it would be to stay with my family in Spain. Only I did not want to leave you on your own, but Trent says not to worry, I must go ahead. He thinks that you too need a break, and he will take you to his house in France.'

Laurel struggled up against the pillows.

'No,' she protested. 'That wouldn't be fair—I'd be a burden to him. He has business deals in Europe to attend to...and...and a life of his own. Can't I go with you, to Spain? I've never been, or met your family.'

Ana shook her head firmly.

'No, *niña*, and now I must tell you why you never have, as I should have told you long ago,' she said. 'Robert always wanted me to tell you, it was I who held back, and now I will honour his wish.'

Laurel was bolt upright and breathless now, her eyes fixed on Ana's face. She had long ago given up hope of ever knowing the truth about her parentage, and now the moment had come, a kind of sick fright had seized her. She wasn't even sure she wanted to know, but there was no retreat from this moment, and she gripped Ana's hand very hard.

'Go on.'

'You are the child of my elder sister, Ysabel,' Ana said quietly. 'She was here in England as a student when she was young, and already engaged to a young man she loved, when foolishly she had a brief affair with a man she met here, and discovered she was pregnant.'

Laurel sat silent for a moment, and then her eyes began to glow with delight.

'So you're my aunt—how fantastic!' she cried. 'We really are related—no wonder people think we look alike; I wish you'd told me years ago!'

'I wish too. But I thought you would want to know your natural mother, and I promised my sister I would protect her secret. She has other children now, Laurel, and none of the family in Spain know anything about what happened to her as a girl,' Ana said in a low voice. 'Laurel, she cannot acknowledge you. This I beg you to accept. Can you do so?'

Laurel was very quiet. She had always known she was adopted, that somewhere in the world was the woman who had given birth to her. At a stroke, Ana had given her that mother—and taken her away again. But she did not hesitate.

'I accept, if you say it must be that way. After all, I had you, and I couldn't have had a more loving mother,' she said quickly. 'But what about this man—couldn't he have married her?'

'He would have, when he learned she was pregnant, but it was her fiancé in Spain she truly loved,' said Ana. 'She sent for me in great distress, for she would not consider an abortion, and I stayed with her until you were born. Even so, she would never tell me who the father was.'

'Then how did my father...I mean, Robert...come into the story?' Laurel frowned.

'Ysabel worked for Robert during her college vacations,' Ana told her. 'He had always been good to her, but I admit I was surprised when he offered to adopt you at birth. A single man with a young child? But his first business was already prospering, and he was in a position to ensure you were well cared for. He arranged the private nursing home and took care of everything. Then Ysabel returned to Spain.'

Ana hesitated. 'Laurel, don't be hurt, but—I think she has blotted from her mind all that happened that year.'

Laurel winced. 'But *you* didn't,' she pointed out.

'I could not,' Ana confessed. 'I felt bound to you, somehow. For a while I was married, but as you know I could not have children myself. Then, when I was widowed, I came back here…only to satisfy myself that you were well and happy…but when I met Robert again, we fell in love.'

Tears came to her eyes at this point, and Laurel pressed her hand. 'Ana, thank you for telling me this. I know it can't have been easy for you.'

'No. But I talked it over with Trent, and he persuaded me that it was right to tell you,' Ana said seriously.

Laurel blinked.

'You told Trent all this?'

'I needed advice. He's *muy simpatico*. You don't mind that he knows? He must have great concern for you, to fly all that way when he heard about Robert…and to come here straight from the airport.'

'He's probably worried about what's happening at Caterplus,' Laurel said embarrassedly, recalling how she had fallen into his arms and sobbed herself to sleep while he held her. 'Milan isn't so far away, after all, and he had an investment to protect.'

'Is it not, then?' Laurel looked up, startled, to see him at the doorway with a tray laden with coffee cups, and an odd gleam in his eyes. 'For your information, madam, I was in Massachusetts, not Milan. Caterplus is quite safe in Alan's capable hands. Furthermore, the day after tomorrow I'm going to Normandy, and you, my girl, are coming with me. No arguments.'

In her exhausted state, her head buzzing with all that Ana had told her, Laurel lacked the mental energy to ask herself why Trent should take time out from his busy schedule and his complex personal life to look after her at this time of crisis. It was enough that he was here, to support and comfort her through the ordeal of the funeral, enough that she had, for the moment, his arm to lean on, and his firm presence at her side.

All the same, it did not feel right simply to take off and leave everything behind her. Alan was more than able enough to cope at Caterplus, she admitted, but—— 'There's Clive,' she had said, thinking aloud. 'What am I to do about him?'

Trent's eyes had darkened momentarily.

'What about Clive?' he demanded. 'Laurel, you can't seriously consider marrying that young man. It's out of the question!'

'I know that.'

A few weeks ago, pride had impelled her to let him think this was at least a possibility. Now she found, amazingly, she had grown beyond such subterfuge.

'The truth is, it was my money he was after, to fund his partnership in a garden centre,' she told him.

Laurel even managed a short, self-mocking laugh, and was rewarded by a gleam of respect in Trent's eyes. How odd—she no longer needed pretence to salve her hurt. She loved Trent, who unfortunately still loved Cara, and there was nothing she could do about it but be grateful for his help and friendship now, when she needed it most.

'If you really think this deal would be the making of him, I'd be prepared to advance Clive a loan,' Trent said thoughtfully. 'That is, if he'd accept it from me. I know I'm not his flavour of the month.'

'He'd accept it from the devil, knowing Clive,' Laurel said wryly. 'But Trent, *why* should you——'

He interrupted her firmly. 'Let's say I like loose ends tied up. Now go and pack, so we can take Ana to the airport and go straight on to catch the ferry.'

As the ferry set sail, and the breeze lifted Laurel's hair from her neck and whipped it around her face, she stole a swift, yearning glance at the man by her side, thankful he was looking out to sea and did not catch her expression.

Loose ends. That was what she was, a loose end to be tied up, comforted and restored to normality, so that he could get back to his real life, his ever-absorbing work and his relentless obsession with the gifted woman who had once been his wife. Laurel was thankful, she was appreciative, but she did not deceive herself.

All the same, something in her spirit lightened and a strange, fleeting happiness washed over her the moment they arrived at the cottage set amid the lush, tranquil pastures, and she thought, I wish I could live here. Here, with him, would be utter heaven. She had no idea how many days he planned on staying, but she would savour every moment of every one, store them up in her memory and relive them gratefully in the years to come.

They ate outside at the table Trent had set out in the garden, and Laurel found she was hungry as she had not been in days. The simple food and country cider were immensely satisfying, and, some spring in her released, she found herself able to talk about Robert, about her life with him and the months leading up to his death, about Ana's revelations about her parentage. She opened

up as she never had to any man, and probably never
would again.

'You mustn't blame yourself for fighting your father
over the Caterplus take-over,' Trent insisted quietly.
'Don't you see—that's the way he loved and preferred
you, his feisty, battling Laurel. Otherwise he'd have told
you about his illness. He didn't *want* you pussyfooting
around him.'

The burden of guilt was lifted from Laurel's shoulders
as she realised that he was right.

'Oh, Trent, that's true! He would have hated it!' she
cried, a smile lighting her face like sunlight breaking
through thunderclouds, her hand reaching out and
catching his. Their eyes met, clung, and Laurel found
she was holding her breath, that once again that special,
shimmering, magical feeling was back with her, the thrill
of anticipatory pleasure, the tremor of desire, the
knowledge that it was all about to happen—just as it
had been that night on the quay at Honfleur. She gazed
into the golden-brown depths of those eyes and said to
herself, *yes*—tonight, if he'll have me, I'm his. I won't
let Cara just reach out and take back casually what she
had once walked away from. I love him, and I'll fight
for him, with every weapon I can summon!

A long moment passed before he let go of her hand
and she said, 'I'll put some coffee on,' and went inside
the cottage.

But she didn't bother with the coffee. Instead she got
out a bottle of Calvados she'd seen earlier in the kitchen
cupboard, and two glasses, and set them on a low table
in the living-room. Then she touched a match to the logs
in the fireplace, and when the wood was beginning to
crackle and burn she went upstairs to the bedroom he'd

designated as hers, and shook out the silk nightdress from her travelling bag.

'Hey,' said Trent, five minutes later as he came indoors, 'have you gone to Brazil to pick the coffee beans?'

And then he stopped, arrested by the sight that met his eyes. The flames leapt and flickered in the twilit room, awakening an answering glimmer in the amber heart of the Calvados in the glasses, and on the dark, shining crown of Laurel's freshly brushed hair. She was curled up on the rug by the fire, the silken nightdress, slit to the thigh, revealing the smooth, fine curve of one leg, the top four buttons undone, half exposing the voluptuous swell of her breasts.

She saw his eyes narrow, heard the soft hiss of his indrawn breath, and knew with a shock of triumph and relief that he did indeed desire her. Well, it was a start, she thought firmly.

'I might be forgiven for assuming,' he said slowly, dropping easily to the rug beside her, 'that you were trying to seduce me.'

She smiled faintly, leaning towards him so that the shift fell open, revealing even more of her body to his gaze.

'I'll forgive you for those lewd thoughts,' she said.

'It's a little foolish to play these games with me, Laurel,' he warned. 'The gentleman in me isn't an automatic function.'

'That's what I'm hoping,' she chuckled.

Suddenly he seized both her shoulders and pulled her towards him, hard.

'Damn you, Laurel,' he groaned, his mouth against her neck, her throat, and then her breast, 'I'm only human! How much of this do you expect me to take?'

Take? Take all of me, she thought blissfully, drowning in the marvellous nearness of him, the urgency of his hands, the near-unstoppable passion of his kisses. She clung to him wildly, offering her lips, her body, all of her young, untried and loving self in return for however much or little of himself he could spare her, and now she had no thought of holding back. She had no thoughts at all.

The air seemed to shake and quiver with the force of his restraint as he put her tenderly but quite firmly aside.

'No, Laurel,' he said roughly, 'this won't do. I want you like crazy, you're driving me mad with wanting you, but not like this, for all the wrong reasons. Not because you're still in shock and reaching out for some kind of comfort! It would have to be because you wanted *me*, and you're not ready for that.'

Tears of despair and anger sprang to her dark eyes.

'I'm as ready as I'll ever be, Trent, as I have been since the first time you touched me!' The furious confession burst out involuntarily, and then she could not stop. 'As ready as I was in the hotel at Honfleur, if only that wretched music hadn't reminded you of Cara, and——'

'Hold on!' he exclaimed, stemming her flow of angry words with an imperious frown. '*What* music?'

She stared at him accusingly.

'You remember? We were... we were just about to make love, when...'

'When you decided it was a little too hot for you, and did a back-flip,' he said ruefully.

'No!' She was sitting back on her heels now, glaring at him. 'Someone was playing *La Bohème*, and you heard it, and... and you lost interest in me...'

'The hell I did!' he retorted indignantly, glaring back. Taking a deep breath, he held up a hand, defusing the moment. 'Laurel, *if* there was music, *if* I was aware of it, I swear it was subconsciously. Music has been part of my deepest being for so long that my response to it is—as necessary as breathing,' he told her. 'That's the only way I can explain it.'

'And Cara? I suppose she's as necessary to you as breathing too!' Laurel retorted.

He waited just a moment before replying, but it was not a hesitation, more a pause for the formulation of an idea he had never expressed in words before.

'Once upon a time, she was,' he said slowly. 'And that kind of closeness leaves a residue, even when there's bitterness. But even at the time, it was partly the music. Cara and the music were bound up together for me, and when she came back it reminded me briefly of all I'd lost when I gave up music and went back to work for my father.'

It took a lot of courage to ask the question, but Laurel knew she had to know the truth of this, once and for all.

'Aren't you still at least a little bit in love with her? You shot off after her to Milan pretty quickly!'

'Laurel, don't you ever *listen*?' he demanded exasperatedly. 'I never went to Milan. I came here to the cottage, because I had some thinking to do, and then I went back to Boston. Since then, I haven't had a waking minute which hasn't been involved with you, and why do you think that is?'

She looked intently into the eyes that were angry and tender at the same time, and her heart lurched wildly. He'd flown straight from Boston to be at her side the minute he'd heard about Robert's death, he'd supported and comforted her through the chaos and anguish and grief of that awful ordeal. He had somehow persuaded Ana to tell her the truth about who she was, to lay the niggling ghost of uncertainty that had troubled her all her life. He'd even advanced Clive the loan to set him on his feet. All this he had done for her. Why?

Because she was a promising young executive he wanted to encourage? Castleford Industries must have many of those, and did he fly halfway round the world for their sakes?

It must mean...it had to mean that...Laurel's hand flew to her mouth to stifle her gasp of astonishment, but it failed utterly.

'I'm trying to tell you I'm in love with you, Laurel,' Trent said. 'I don't know when or how it happened, but on the night you told me Clive had asked you to marry him I realised that if there were the slightest chance of that happening my life would fall apart.'

'Oh, darling!' Laurel all but fell into his arms. 'There was never, ever the slightest chance! I knew I loved you after we came back from Normandy, but I thought I'd thrown away my chance, and that you were still hung up on Cara!'

He shook his head. 'I realised, when I met her again recently, that Cara is an illusion,' he said. 'On stage, she may be sublime, but off stage, she doesn't really exist.'

Suddenly his face was serious.

'Laurel, let's get married, here in France, very quietly and as soon as possible,' he urged. 'It's too soon after the funeral for a big wedding, and Ana may well stay in Spain for some time. I love you and I can't wait to put a ring on your finger and make sure you're mine! I don't think Robert would mind, or think it irreverent of us.'

'Robert would be delighted,' Laurel murmured, 'and so would I, my love.' Already her heart had begun to race joyfully at the thought of a quiet wedding here in the serene heart of Normandy, and the two of them coming back to this cottage as man and wife. 'But your father... what would *he* say?'

Trent laughed softly.

'He'll agree with what my mother told him—that it was high time I was settled down, and the quicker the better!'

Seeing her puzzled expression, he said, '*She* was the one I went to Boston to see. I told her I'd met a girl I loved, and I intended to marry her, even if it meant depriving my father of a first-rate manager—at least for the next few years! I told her this girl was driving me wild, and I'd have her for my wife whatever it took! That something in me was sure she loved me, if only I could get her to realise it.'

Laurel's upturned face was the face of a woman in love, eyes shining with a serene certainty, but a hint of girlishness lingered as her teeth nipped gently at her lower lip.

'This girl... are you really sure that she loves you?' she asked, with a smile that was utterly and intentionally provocative. 'Perhaps she needs a little... er... persuasion?'

Without a moment's hesitation, Trent lowered her to the ground, his hands pinioning hers so that she could not have escaped, his mouth seeking hers, demanding a surrender she was only too willing to give.

'I intend to take that as a challenge, lady,' he murmured against the warm skin of her throat.

'Oh, I sincerely hope you will, my love,' she said.

Outside, the night sky darkened, and in the cottage, the flames of the fire subsided into glowing embers, but neither of them noticed. They were lost in love.

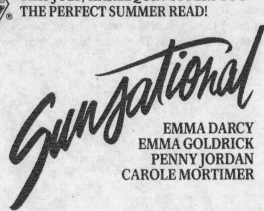

Back by Popular Demand

Janet Dailey
Americana

A romantic tour of America through fifty favorite Harlequin Presents, each set in a different state researched by Janet and her husband, Bill. A journey of a lifetime in one cherished collection.

In August, don't miss the exciting states featured in:

Title #13 — ILLINOIS
The Lyon's Share

#14 — INDIANA
The Indy Man

Available wherever Harlequin books are sold.

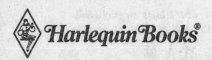
Harlequin Books®

GREAT NEWS...
HARLEQUIN UNVEILS NEW SHIPPING PLANS

For the convenience of customers, Harlequin has announced that Harlequin romances will now be available in stores at these convenient times each month*:

Harlequin Presents, American Romance, Historical, Intrigue:

> May titles: April 10
> June titles: May 8
> July titles: June 5
> August titles: July 10

Harlequin Romance, Superromance, Temptation, Regency Romance:

> May titles: April 24
> June titles: May 22
> July titles: June 19
> August titles: July 24

We hope this new schedule is convenient for you.

With only two trips each month to your local bookseller, you'll never miss any of your favorite authors!

*Please note: There may be slight variations in on-sale dates in your area due to differences in shipping and handling.

*Applicable to U.S. only.

HDATES-RR